# *the* house around *the* corner

ELIZABETH
BROMKE

Cover design by Red Leaf Cover Design

THE HOUSE AROUND THE CORNER
Publishing in the Pines
White Mountains, Arizona

# NOTE TO THE READER

Welcome to Harbor Hills! I'm so happy you're here. You're about to begin the third book in the Harbor Hills saga. Although this story can stand on its own, you may want to consider reading books one and two first, in order to avoid spoilers for those stories and to get to know the characters. Book one is *The House on Apple Hill Lane*. Book two is *The House with the Blue Front Door*. Each available widely!

If you've already read the first two books or are ready to continue, here is a brief synopsis to remind you where the ladies are at the start of this story.

*Quinn Whittle* and her teen daughter, Vivi, have settled into 696 Apple Hill Lane, but Quinn feels the dread of a new, unnamed problem. She can't pin it down, but fortunately, she has a new distraction to keep her from overfocusing on her unebbing compulsions: Forrest Jericho, her boss. But that distraction may be the very problem she fears. While Quinn is daydreaming about the handsome newspaper editor, what is her teenage daughter up to?

*Jude Banks* is teaching at Hills High and enjoying her routines with her cat, Liebchen. Sometimes, she gets the feeling that her neighbors are a little *much*. Too dramatic. Too gossipy. But they are still her best friends—her only friends. Until an unlikely suitor pursues the enigmatic divorcée.

*Annette Best* and her husband and son are prepping their house for sale. They've got a place to go and a loose plan for turning around their finances. Meanwhile, Annette's son, Elijah, is dating the neighbor-girl, Vivi. The two are inseparable. Until they set about a project in the backyard, where a worrisome discovery wedges itself into their fledgling romance.

After struggling with the recent deaths of her husband and daughter, *Beverly Castle* finds some closure. She learns that her daughter was not texting and driving ahead of the icy, tragic car crash. Instead, Beverly's husband had used the teenager's phone to contact his affair partner. After coming to terms with the shocking revelation, Beverly can now dive into a new phase of her career: a brand-new newspaper column for locals—something useful and a little bit thrilling.

*The unnamed girl* has become an *unnamed woman*,

and she is finally ready to revisit Apple Hill Lane and her grandparents. But when she arrives at the ramshackle family home, something is wrong. Nana is dead, and it's up to the woman to help Grandad bury a troublesome secret.

*Happy reading!*

*Yours,*
*Elizabeth Bromke*

# PROLOGUE

The bright-white clouds of summer had long since curdled into pillows of cottage cheese, sailing over Michigan. They'd left, going wherever clouds go. The next town or up higher into the ether. Then again, the girl wondered if clouds were more the sort to *change* rather than to *leave*.

Anyway, new clouds had taken the place of those summer ones. Autumnal clouds: sometimes dark, sometimes wispy. Sucking in orange from the sun and casting dusky shadows across Harbor Hills.

The girl wondered, too, if *she* was the sort to change rather than leave altogether. Maybe she—who once was a warm, contented child—had turned gloomy and dense and heavy with the shift in seasons. With age.

Fifteen years had passed since her last visit to Apple Hill Lane. *That* visit.

By this time, the girl wasn't a girl any longer. She was a fully-fledged woman who'd established a career and even a name for herself. And now, as such—as a broody, edgy woman—she'd become a mess of nerves. Antsy and unmoored. All the time.

Presently, Thanksgiving emerged in the forecast. For many years now, she'd found little pockets where she could spend holidays. Mostly at church or with church acquaintances. When she was quite younger, there were girlfriends and boyfriends who took her in. Never a best friend, though. And never a serious boyfriend.

She was tired of those trivial, fleeting relationships. However, loneliness wasn't a welcome replacement for a lack of the meaningful ties that every other young woman and man seemed to build. And for the *woman*, spending another holiday with veritable strangers would serve only to make things worse in her troubled mind. So, come late November, she crept out on the fragile limb of a birch. So to speak. Hadn't Frost said something about this? *One could do worse than be a swinger of birches*?

Well, indeed, one *could* do worse, and the woman had.

She'd done far, far worse, of course. Her whole life had been spent on the so-called ground, flat-footed. Instead of swinging on birches, risking the fall, she'd stayed rooted to a risk-free and depressing tedium of nothing. Work and home. Home and work. Everything in her world blurred together.

But this holiday season, she'd committed to venturing up the trunk of a tree and out on a bendy limb. Maybe she'd fall and break her neck and plunge to hell. Maybe she'd smile and laugh and swing to heaven.

So, after packing a modest suitcase, the woman drove. Not home. She'd never call it home. Home was still a floating, ambiguous, abstract concept—like a feather on the wind, loosed from its avian host and drifting anywhere. Home was not a real place. Not for the girl who had become a woman.

She drove and she drove until she found herself there, along the curb in front of 696 Apple Hill Lane.

Smoothing her dress—an ankle-length, olive-colored linen number with beige buttons from breastbone to bottom—she closed her car door. Under the dress, she wore a beige mock turtleneck. Over it, a denim jacket. Those three layers coupled with a pair of black tights helped shield her against the November chill. She also wore a hat that day. A denim bucket hat to match the jacket. The brim folded itself back, exposing her wispy bangs—lighter, presently, with the help of a little Sun In.

She hadn't called ahead.

Junk littered the front yard. Rusted tools leaned at odd angles against the garage door, as if set like booby traps. Wet and rotting boxes sank into the overgrown grass. Good thing there wasn't an HOA to contend with. Grandad's windows would be taped over in notices.

She lifted the hem of her dress and picked her way through the weedy yard and up to the front door, which she rapped tentatively with her knuckles. After a moment, when no one answered, she knocked again, harder.

The noise of movement from within was readily perceptible, and she swayed back, swallowing then forcing a breath up from her chest.

The door swung open, and a very old man appeared inside the threshold. He made a grunt.

Studying him, the woman saw that, though he'd aged, he was very much the same. White hair combed neatly over. Thick glasses, foggy, pushed to the very top of the bridge of his nose. His eyebrows, white and wild, poked down over the glass lenses. He wore a plaid, long-sleeved button-down with suspenders and soft-looking, gray wool pants. Rubber-footed shoes glued him to the floor, but still he leaned heavily on a gnarled, waxen stick—a cane.

When it became clear that the grunt was as much of a greeting as he'd offer, the woman stammered a response. "I—um, it's *me*." She blinked and swallowed. "It's me, Grandad?"

She didn't mean it as a question, but this was the

force he held over her, even now, so many years after she'd last seen him.

The very old man squinted behind his glasses and bent forward before rocking back again. "Oh, my," he said on a wheeze. "Oh, come in. Come on, now. Come *in*." He waddled backward and she did as she was told, her heart racing in her chest at the warm reception.

Surprisingly, she felt comfortable. Maybe it was the stacks of newspapers or rows of filing cabinets. The blankets and furniture crowding around them making her feel, in a way, safe.

"Tea? Coffee?" His age receded somehow, and he did away with the cane and stoop, like it had been an act.

She nodded eagerly. "Either."

He set about heating water in the microwave and shaking a single plastic pack of instant coffee into two mugs, splitting one serving across both. After adding a heaping spoonful of sugar to each, he passed one her way. She pretended to enjoy it as they sat at the kitchen table. Rather, they sat *near* the kitchen table, their knees touching as they cradled their mugs on their laps, unable to use the table itself because of its mess.

She asked after him. He asked after her. They caught up.

After they agreed the woman would stay through the holiday, she found the courage to say the thing that she had never expressed to him. "Um." She cleared her throat. Her eyes fell to the ground. At that point, it hadn't yet been covered in layers of oriental rugs and runners. It was just the wood floor. Unpolished but unadorned, too. "So, were you able to finish the...*thing*?"

With a man like Grandad, one might expect him to be confused at such vagueries as *finish* and *thing*.

But Grandad wasn't a confused sort. "I managed." He slurped his drink and tried for a smile when she finally looked back up at him.

"I'm sorry, you know." Swallowing a tiny sip, she ran a tongue over her bottom lip, lizard-like. "That I couldn't...*help*." And she was, too. After all the money he'd sent. All the letters and cards and attempts he'd made to be all that a grandad ought to be. She was sorry.

"Oh. 'S all right," he drawled in that old-timey Midwestern brogue. "Wasn't much of a to-do, anyhow."

"Oh." She took another tiny sip. "Maybe we could visit her together? I'd like to pay my respects. Even now."

"Maybe," he mumbled, sputtering through a wrong-pipe swallow of his coffee. He hacked for a bit, and she waited.

"Are you okay?"

Nodding and clearing his throat, he went on. "It's not like she's alone or anything."

The woman cocked her head and lifted her

eyebrows. "She's not alone?" She looked past him through the small box window at the back of the kitchen.

He shook his head and coughed again. "Didn't get to mention it, but the whole family's out there, you know." He threw his head over his right shoulder and toward the deeper, back section of the neighborhood.

She was reminded of a discovery she'd made at a church friend's house in a nearby town. A single, cracked grave marker in the girl's very backyard. It was overgrown with weeds, the name meaningless even to the family who lived there. In Michigan, these little morbid stones weren't unheard of. Outhouses and errant tombstones speckled the rural areas of the region, many dating back to the late 1700s.

"Oh, right." She nodded like she understood, but this was a tradition that the woman did *not* understand. Not in modern times. People didn't bury family in their own backyards in *modern* times. Then again, Grandad didn't say it was the backyard.

Curiouser by the minute, the woman asked, "Where exactly did you put her?" She felt heat invade her neck. "I mean—where is her *plot*? Exactly?"

"Plot?" he sputtered. "They're all out there." He jutted his chin again over his shoulder. "The land there. Around the corner."

## CHAPTER 1—VIVI

In the Best family's backyard, Vivi and Elijah stood, frozen. For a while, they simply gawked at the mud-encrusted bone that poked itself up out of the ground, beneath what once was Eli Best's childhood fort. As they stared, amazed and confused and horrified, the dog continued pawing with a hunger at the soft, damp grave. None the wiser, Sadie had unearthed a generous chunk of, well, *skeleton*.

"It's a femur," Elijah said at last, turning and inspecting that first-found bone in his hand like a kid inspecting a new, unfamiliar toy.

Vivi sighed. "Yeah. I think so." Next to a skull or complete set of finger bones or maybe even a rib, the femur was the most readily recognizable human bone to a teenager. Or, at least, to a teenager who was in first-semester sophomore biology class.

"Sadie," Elijah hissed, breaking from their shared trance. He patted his thigh with his free hand, and the dog jogged over, panting excitedly. "Kennel," he directed her, pointing toward the house.

Sadie whined. "Sadie, *kennel*," he repeated. The dog shook her golden coat, and dirt sprayed out. Vivi squeezed her eyes shut and tried to twist away before specks of earth painted her shirt and skin and hair. Too late, she wiped her face with both hands and the backs of her wrists, smearing off the evidence of their discovery.

Giving up on Sadie, Elijah turned to face Vivi. "What do we do?"

"What do *we* do?" she answered, wide eyed. "It's *your* backyard."

"You say that like it's *my* skeleton."

Vivi shrugged. "Maybe it's your parents'?"

Elijah shook his head. "My parents don't bury bodies in the backyard." He added, "Anyway, this one seems to be way old."

"As old as the fort?" Vivi asked.

"Who knows?" He grimaced and stared at the wreckage—both that of the fort and that of the, well, *person*.

"Anyway," Vivi reasoned, "it wouldn't be your *mom's*. She's the one who made us take down the fort. If she knew what was under—"

"Yeah." Elijah was quick to agree.

"Who decided to build the fort *there*?" Vivi pointed to the small square lot at the back corner of the yard. The same place where she'd sought shelter just months earlier. Where Elijah had offered her refuge. It was a...gravesite. She shuddered.

Elijah pitched the bone back to its shallow hole. Then again, how shallow was it? His dad had put in a decently deep concrete footer. They'd figured that out quickly enough. "I don't remember." He scratched his head then crossed his arms. "I was little."

Vivi blinked, shifted her weight. Her body trembled, though she wasn't sure if it was excitement or the chill in the early October air.

Elijah noticed and tugged her to him, wrapping his arms around her back.

They'd hugged before. Something quick at school between classes. On the day Vivi ran away. Maybe one or two other times, but this one was different.

Their bodies pressed together, and a light breeze tickled the hair at the back of her neck. She felt Eli's heartbeat in her own chest—or was that hers? "What do we do now?" Vivi whispered into his hoodie. He smelled good, like he'd just had a shower. And swiped on men's deodorant. And a spritz of his dad's cologne maybe. Or maybe Eli had his own cologne. When had he started wearing cologne? Vivi shook the thought.

He answered above her head, but she heard his voice through its vibrations in his body—and in hers. "We tell my mom."

Vivi reared back. "She's going to *flip*."

## CHAPTER 2—ANNETTE

Once the yard sale was long over and dusk started to fall across Harbor Hills, Annette Best and her husband, Roman, returned into their house. The place was a shell of its former glory.

At least, that's how a nearly empty house was *supposed* to feel, like something lesser. Like...not so much a home anymore. But somehow, even with boxes lining the rooms and everything pulled from the walls, there was little real difference. This confounded Annette. She'd decorated, of course. She'd been icily particular and careful in her decorations, treating her house like a model home, staging it, tweaking it for the seasons. That way, if a client ever stepped inside, that client would see just what exceptional taste Annette had. And if Annette had exceptional taste in her home, this would naturally transfer to the homes she sold.

Right?

But now—now that this model-home house of hers was packed and ready for the next occupant, Annette had to wonder where the *home* part of her home had gone?

Had it ever existed to begin with?

Roman kissed her chastely on the cheek. "I've got some closing paperwork to finish and print. We both need to sign it for Monday. And the Becketts do, too."

Monday. Moving Day.

"I can walk it over to them tonight or tomorrow?" she offered. The Becketts, the family with whom they were swapping houses, lived kitty-corner behind the Best property, in a little red cottage-style home. It was far smaller than Annette's current colonial on Apple Hill. And the street name was different, too. Her new address would be 697 Dogwood Drive. In every single way, the move felt like a downgrade. Smaller house. Less charming address. And, most egregiously, she wouldn't be with her girlfriends. She'd be *behind* them.

Still, the deal was their redemption. Annette reminded herself that it wasn't a down*grade*, it was a down*size*. And wasn't downsizing, like, a trend these days, anyway? Marie Kondo and minimalism and simplify and all that? Annette made a mental note to read up on the craze.

And Dogwood wasn't so bad. Despite being the very backyard of Apple Hill, Dogwood had a more rural effect to it. Middle America. Though a tad less *Americana*, which Annette had tried to brand herself as. That was part of the inspiration behind their company name, Best on the Block. Red, White, and Blue. The American way—all things great and *best*. And living on a street named Apple Hill Lane—what could be more American?

Come Monday, however, Annette would be an outsider to that life.

Roman turned at the hallway before disappearing into his office—one of two rooms that still had anything in it. "Oh and—my parents are coming to town after the move."

Annette froze. "What? *Why?*" Annette loved her in-laws as much as the next person, but now wasn't the time to host family.

"I invited them. They'll stay at Bertie's, don't worry, Ann."

It didn't matter if they were staying at Bertie's B&B. Annette knew how this would go. Mimi Best wasn't much for relaxation. If she was coming to town...she'd be *around*.

"But *why*?" Annette propped her hands on her hips. "Roman, we're *moving*. And...the business—now's...not a good time. We're in flux."

"I know," Roman answered, leaning against the

door frame, his hands gripping it on either side—bracing to say the next thing. "But I figured they could help."

Annette was speechless. The last thing she wanted was the interference of the Bests. Sure, they were real estate titans. No, she didn't want their help.

Roman didn't wait for a reply. Typical Roman.

She was suddenly grateful the guest room mattress leaned against the foyer wall, ready for moving. Maybe she'd topple it to the floor and sleep there instead of on the air mattress Roman had inflated for their last two nights on Apple Hill.

Taking a long, deep breath, Annette forced herself into Roman's shoes. He loved his parents. He saw their success. He was a *product* of it, even. He trusted them to come and save Annette and Elijah and their problems. It wasn't Roman's fault if Mimi could be difficult. And anyway, if Annette's mother were closer—physically or emotionally—you could bet your bottom dollar Annette would be lassoing her down to Harbor Hills, too. In fact, Annette hoped that one day she'd get a call from Elijah asking for her to come save him.

The return of the in-laws was only natural.

She let out her breath and frowned.

Where *was* Elijah?

## CHAPTER 3—ANNETTE

Annette stalked to the backyard, where she'd assigned Elijah to finish dismantling his childhood fort.

This, naturally, had hatched an argument. *The new family would love to have a fort, Mom!*

She didn't disagree, but *Roman* had built the fort, and Roman didn't care about things like splinters and exposed screw tips that could score a child's delicate skin. He hadn't *had* to know about such things. It had always been Annette who scraped Elijah's skin with tweezers until the sliver of wood emerged. Or lie to him that the rubbing alcohol wouldn't hurt, not one bit, before cleaning his wounds like an army medic, bandaging and sending him back out to war.

Sometimes, Annette wondered if Roman's absence in these more intimate moments of parenting had turned Elijah against his father. There wasn't a hatred there. Not even an indifference. But there was a chip. An edge. For both men, actually.

Annette now wished she'd assigned Roman to deconstruct the old fort. It was *his* mess. Why make Elijah do it? Maybe Annette was part of the problem in the clash between her husband and their son.

Back inside, she glanced out the window and she saw that the fort—what was *once* the fort—remained as a heap of wood. Elijah hadn't finished tossing the aged lumber into the hopper she'd ordered for just such an occasion. Most of it lay like shattered glass at odd angles over the mound. A shovel stuck out of the dirt in one place. A pickax in another. Sadie was tearing into the soft soil that had lain in wait all those years.

Annette set her jaw and swung the door open. "Sadie, *come*!" she barked to the dog, clapping her thighs.

Sadie ignored her and continued a puppy-frantic pawing at the earth.

Annette ventured through the open door and over the threshold. The light of the sinking sun had begun to transfer itself to the moon, like an exchange of power. Night was ready for its shift, but Sadie was digging like a vampire's minion and Elijah and Vivi weren't anywhere in the yard. Not that Annette could see.

"Elijah!" she called then returned her attention to Sadie. "Sadie, *come*," Annette hissed, glancing toward her neighbor's fence. Maybe the pair had called it a night and had taken to Vivi's bedroom, where they had relatively more privacy. One parent to duck away from rather than two. Then again, Roman could hardly count as a supervisory presence in the Best home.

The temperature had dropped since the yard sale. Though it had been cold that morning, a deeper chill hit Annette now. She wrapped her plum-colored knit sweater tighter over her torso, feeling her midsection roll over her pant waist. Annette pushed off that concern for those of the present.

"Mom."

Annette jerked forward, nearly losing her footing in the grass. She spun around, her hand pressed against her chest, her heart racing. "Eli*jah*." She let out his name with the breath she'd been holding.

Two figures stood on the porch, the lamplight behind them casting each in shadow. Vivi was with him. Annette breathed again then let out a short laugh. She turned back to Sadie, and the whole of the backyard suddenly seemed less dark. Sadie, less frantic. Annette, less frightened. "Sadie! *Come!*"

As Annette repeated her command, Elijah gave a sharp whistle. Sadie's floppy, golden ears, browned in mud, twitched up and the dog gave Elijah her attention. "Sadie, *come*," he added, and Sadie half galloped, half lumbered his way, her tongue lolling out of her mouth as Elijah crouched down and scratched beneath her collar.

"Mrs. Best," Vivi spoke up. The funny thing about Vivi, Annette always thought, was how she was much less of a girl than Elijah was a boy. She had a grown-upness to her that often positioned her, in Annette's mind, as Quinn's younger sister, rather than daughter. At first, when Elijah and Vivi had connected, Annette had been thrilled. Her son hadn't shown much interest in girls before then. Now that, in and of itself, wasn't any cause for concern. What did worry Annette was Elijah's ability to connect with *anyone* at all.

Not since Kayla's death.

Since they were kids, Elijah and Kayla had been glued at the hip. Nothing romantic, no. Just best friends, in the purest sense. When the accident happened, Elijah had shut himself in. His other friends had only offered so much patience. They, with the rest of the high school, moved on in a matter of weeks. Maybe even one week. High school tragedies like Kayla's were memorable, sure, but the collective teenage mind was restless, and teenagers themselves, self-interested.

Elijah didn't have that problem, not after Kayla's death.

So, when Vivi showed up, bright and shiny and

new and *lonely*, Annette had been excited. Maybe she'd help her son in a way she, as a mom, just couldn't.

Then, the two became just as inseparable or more, and Annette's hope turned to...

Something else.

"Yes?" Annette met Vivi's icy stare.

"We found this."

That was the first moment Annette's eyes found their way to the object in the girl's hands, laid across like a platter. An offering.

"What is it?" Annette leaned in, peering with curiosity.

"It's a human femur," Elijah answered. Sadie had begun to whine. "Sadie dug it up. She's working on..." He trailed off and stared where the dog had begun to pull back toward—the old, felled fort.

Annette's hand flew from her chest to her mouth.

"Oh my God," she whispered.

The next question, naturally, was *whose*? Whose femur?

But this wasn't the question that Annette asked. Because regardless of whose femur—after all, that person was dead—the problem was much more urgent. The problem was a legal one.

And the problem could cripple the Best family's real estate deal.

Annette acted quickly. "Where were you two? Just now? Why was Sadie still out there, digging?"

"I had to go to the bathroom," Elijah answered.

"I went to Eli's room to use his computer," Vivi added.

"Use his computer for *what*?" Annette shot back.

"To look up pictures of human femurs?" she replied, that snotty, precocious tone undercutting the question in her voice.

Annette set her jaw. "Okay." She gave a nod, thinking. *Thinking*.

"Mom," Elijah interrupted. "What should we do?"

"First of all, kennel Sadie, for the love of God." A headache hatched its pulse in the soft hollow at the back of her neck. She rubbed it. *Thinking*.

Vivi asked, "Then what?"

Annette blinked, looked at her. The girl's eyes were twice as wide as normal. Her arms frozen beneath the grotesque evidence. Evidence of what, though? Annette wasn't sure, anyhow. Maybe Vivi wasn't so bad. She was holding a human femur, after all. Maybe Vivi was tough. Annette needed a tough ally right now.

"Then I'll talk to Roman," Annette replied, coating her voice in assurance.

"Mom," Elijah cut in, his hand tight around Sadie's collar. "Shouldn't we"—he dropped his voice—"*call the police?*"

Annette's stomach twisted, zapping the appetite she thought she'd have for that last slice of pizza in the fridge. Zapping her energy, too. And her unfounded ire for Sadie and Elijah and Vivi. "Oh, honey," she replied, huffing a breath, her voice cracking as she tried to switch gears—to undo her panic and set a better example. "There's no reason to call the police." A little, shrill laugh spilled from the back of her throat. "No reason!" A shaky smile shaped her mouth. "It's just...an old..."

"What?" Elijah's face darkened.

Annette licked her lips.

Vivi shifted the bone in her hands, lowering it as if bored now.

Annette shrugged and answered calmly, "It's probably nothing."

## CHAPTER 4—JUDE

Night after night for the past decade—longer, really—Jude Banks had had a routine.

Grapefruit or cantaloupe in her eat-in kitchen by five. Sometimes, she'd add a side of chips and salsa.

Brisk walk up to Crabtree Court, all the way to the back of the community, then back home.

Feed Liebchen.

Hot bubble bath *or* shower—alternating nights—with shaving duty every third night when that night was a shower night. Any more frequently and Jude ran the risk of incorrigible razor burn.

Television with Liebchen and half a glass of Syrah. Popcorn if she was in a mood.

Book in bed until she started drifting.

It was this, and nothing else.

Even when Gene was around, and even if they were on the boat or elsewhere, Jude would emulate this routine to the best of her ability. In the past several months, it had cemented itself more, particularly now that Liebchen was sold on it. Should Jude stray, she'd pay overnight with a grumpy Liebchen knocking perfume bottles from the vanity and yowling like a cat in heat, rather than tame, quiet Liebchen.

That Saturday night—that autumn-crisp night with the first smells of woodsmoke curling in through the cracked window—Liebchen growled at her from his perch atop the armoire as Jude sat at her vanity, a smattering of makeup spilled across its top.

All this because of one handyman, too.

After their appointment to go over her renovation requests, all Dean Jericho was supposed to do was tuck his clipboard under his arm, shake her hand, and leave to run numbers on some arcane, dust-mottled calculator in a trailer-office. Send her back an estimation within forty-eight hours.

That was supposed to be *it*.

But then he'd lingered at her front door talking over paint colors. Paint colors! She really ought to consider eggshell finish rather than matte, since it hides imperfections—like a child's muddy hand trailing down the wall. He'd laughed at this image. She'd bristled. "This house is practically a museum," she'd retorted, snorting to soften her blow. "I mean—

there just isn't going to be a lot of mess one way or the other around here. And isn't matte more tasteful?"

Inane, really. The whole conversation was fundamentally *inane*, but then, it wasn't about paint finish, was it?

She'd grown impatient and finally given in. "Fine. Eggshell!" Then, she'd thrown her hands up and tried for light laughter, but her top lip—red with lipstick—caught on her canine and had probably smudged red down the whole tooth. This had forced Jude to pretend to laugh even harder and more awkwardly, thereby allowing her to cover her mouth with her hand to hide the personal foible. Dean had stood there, grinning at her like a fool himself.

Jude had given one more laugh behind her hand and with the other had gestured through the open front door—an indication for him to *leave*.

Instead, though, he'd leaned into the door frame, his wide grin slipping into a playful smirk.

She'd frowned and behind her hand had run her tongue over her top teeth like a squeegee. Satisfied enough not to melt into the floor, she'd raised her eyebrows and smiled, closed lipped. Then Jude had folded her arms over her chest and cocked her head, waiting for him.

Dean had cleared his throat, pushed off of the doorway, and shoved his hands into his pockets. "Jude," he'd said, his sparkling blue eyes landing on hers and holding them there in a trance, "what are you doing tonight?"

She still been worried about the lipstick-on-the-tooth situation, or else she'd have had an answer so fast, ol' Dean Jericho would have fallen on his tight, jeans-clad butt on her welcome mat. Swallowing and giving her top row one more pass with her tongue, she'd said at last, "My usual." It was honest, after all.

"Does your usual include dinner at the Dorgendorf?"

"The Dorgendorf?" Jude had answered. The Dorgendorf was an age-old restaurant in the very heart of town. It anchored the hub of where Main Street crossed with Hill Road, a corner restaurant born when the town was settled in the late 1800s. For a long while, Jude knew, it had been called Oma's. Descendants of Oma Dorgendorf had opted for an overhaul at one point. Jude understood this happened in the '80s, when chic was in and downhome was out. So, Oma's business faded into the annals of local history as one of her brood decided he could make something of Harbor Hills yet.

"Sure. The Dorgendorf." Dean's answer had come through a crooked smile and a shrug of his shoulders.

Jude had then stiffened. Had she given him a signal that she was interested? Because she most *certainly* was not interested.

So, why then, come five o'clock on Saturday night,

had she showered on a bath night, shaved a day early, and skipped her fruit and her walk and stood in front of her full-length mirror while Liebchen batted at the leg of her apple-red skinny jeans?

Why?

She checked her wristwatch—still early!—chewed her bottom lip, and frowned at Liebchen.

Then Jude grabbed her phone from the vanity and tapped on his assigned name: *Dean Jericho—Electrician.*

They hadn't exchanged one single message about tonight. For all she knew, he'd pranked her and wasn't planning to pick her up at all! Then again, he had said it. Clear as day. *I'll be back at six.*

"Oh no you won't," Jude murmured wickedly, her eyebrow arched. She read aloud the message for Liebchen's benefit and that of proofing. *I'm very sorry, but can we raincheck?*

Jude had learned it was best not to give a false excuse. Otherwise, she could very well contradict herself.

Her heart returned to its normal thudding. Her breaths softened, and the sweat along her spine turned cold. It was the right decision.

She peeled her jeans off, tugged her shirt over her head, and lay the outfit across the foot of her bed before sitting back down at her vanity to undo the makeup and curse herself for giving up her routine for a *man*. And one she hardly knew, at that. She could already feel the razor burn festering along her shins. She could hear the growl in her stomach.

Mostly, though, Jude could feel the emptiness in her house. The void that she'd allowed it to become. The cavern she'd curated out of heartache and self-preservation.

Mostly, Jude felt lonely.

## CHAPTER 5—QUINN

Monday morning, Quinn Whittle had a meeting with Forrest, her boss and the editor of the *Harbor Herald*.

First things first, however. It was her day to drive Vivi and Elijah to school. The carpool had been Annette's idea, naturally. Sure, the kids could take the bus, but in Harbor Hills, that would mean sharing the bus with the elementary school. Sharing with the elementary school meant waking up an extra hour early, and for a teenager, there was no such thing as waking up an extra hour early. Not if you had the luxury of a parent or a neighbor.

So, until the following school year, when the two would officially have their driver's licenses and dedicated parking spots in the Hills High lot, Quinn would cover Mondays and Wednesdays, and Annette would cover Tuesdays and Thursdays. Fridays were up to Roman. Quinn learned that Roman was a Friday sort of dad. The opposite of Matt, who'd been crushed to lose Vivi for an entire five days at a time and doubly so when his *little girl* begged off the weekend visits in favor of nursing her local social life.

Roman seemed older than Matt, too. More traditional. More business-y. A little removed from his own life, maybe. And there was something in that that entranced Quinn. The ability to...not care. Or, at least, appear as such.

Meanwhile Quinn had started slipping back into some old bad habits. She'd carted in five bottles of bleach just the Saturday before, after the yard sale. Yard sales were beginning to give her the heebie-jeebies—though why, she wasn't sure. She'd stayed up Saturday night until one in the morning, scrubbing on her hands and knees. Vivi had entered sometime before then. Quinn hadn't stopped to check the clock, only to warn Vivi to deposit her shoes and go directly to the shower.

"The shower? Mom, it's *late*," Vivi had whined.

"You were working a *yard sale* today, Viv. And then in Elijah's yard? Please—take a shower."

"I'll wash my hands and face," Vivi had snapped back, mounting the staircase toward her bedroom.

Quinn's skin had crawled. "Just, *please*, Vivi. Shower. Okay? For me?"

Even as she'd said the words, she knew they were ridiculous. Controlling. Yada, yada. But *knowing* those things didn't change her compulsion to make such demands. "Please, Viv," Quinn had begged in a quiet voice. Desperate.

"It's starting again," Vivi had said. "Why?"

"No, it's not." Quinn had sniffled and rubbed the back of her yellow rubber glove across her forehead, pushing damp tendrils of hair off her damp skin. "I'm just having a bad day."

Vivi had leaned into the bannister and narrowed her eyes on her mother. "Why?"

"I don't know. I don't...know." And she didn't. Well, she *did*. But it was intangible things. The imminent Homecoming dance, for starters. Vivi wanted to hire a limo. She wanted to have her hair and makeup done professionally. They weren't *there* yet. Maybe they'd never be.

Not only that, but Annette was moving. Quinn hadn't come to know the Becketts yet, but she knew they weren't as family oriented as their lifestyle might otherwise suggest.

Sometimes at night, after their toddler was in bed, the husband—Tad—would have a group of friends over for a barbecue. They'd roar into laughter together, then it'd be quiet. Then another roar. It would go on like that until Quinn moved from her bedroom at the back of the second floor to the sofa in the front room.

Now this family would be right next door. Would it get worse? The fun-having?

That was when it had occurred to Quinn that she wasn't one for fun. This would've been fine and dandy if she were still living alone, but Vivi's friend group was growing to be larger than just Elijah. At least, that's how Homecoming plans sounded. Like a little group of girls Vivi had enmeshed with in some of her classes.

But see, Quinn was pleased to entertain Vivi's friends. It wasn't Vivi's fun that irritated Quinn. It was...something else. It was everything out of Quinn's control—her finances and her property lines and the fact that the one woman who'd been very much a rock was now little more than a rowboat, adrift in the neighborhood and maybe even unhappy in her life.

So, anxiety had crept back in, and Quinn batted at it with whatever tools she had—which were usually bleach and rags and yellow rubber gloves.

But Vivi was unlike Quinn's mother, who had always indulged her. Vivi had stomped up the stairs and called over her shoulder, "I'll shower tomorrow."

Quinn gritted her teeth. Her shoulders tensed and deep pain whipped like a cord up the back of her neck. This meant Quinn would have to clean Vivi's sheets on Sunday, and that would be *fine* if she hadn't already washed the sheets on Friday thinking she'd get ahead of the long weekend.

She sank to the floor and squeezed her eyes shut,

willing away the misplaced anger. Fighting hard for that moment of acceptance to wash over her. And come one o'clock, it would. Fitfully in a poor sleep on the sofa since Tad and his young dad friends were cracking beers and jokes like they didn't have a care in the world. Not a toddler sleeping upstairs. Not a pregnant wife. Not a big move on Monday. Not a neighbor with a bad case of obsessive-compulsive disorder who couldn't stand the sounds of their fun and laughter.

But now it was Monday, and Monday mornings were a welcome reprieve from the downtime of the weekend. And despite the fact that it prolonged her journey to the office, Quinn enjoyed driving the kids to school. It was important and good. The sort of thing a very good mother did. The best kind. Driving her daughter to school.

"You two have that report due today, right?" She glanced in the rearview to catch the look Vivi and Elijah exchanged. Quinn frowned. "Did you finish?" she asked, reading their guilty faces.

"Yes!"

"No."

Their answers crashed together—Vivi's lie loud and sharp and Elijah's truth low and dull.

"Um." Quinn glanced again to catch Vivi's face in the rearview. "I thought you were working on it all day yesterday? That's why you couldn't help Annette with loading the wood?" Annette had been paying the two to dismantle and haul off Elijah's childhood fort. She'd been worried it was a potential liability. If the Beckett toddler climbed inside, he could poke himself with a rusty nail. Or worse.

"My mom and dad are handling the wood," Elijah answered for Vivi.

Quinn let up on the gas and coasted down Schoolhouse Street toward the drop-off circle out front of the school. Idling behind a line of SUVs—Harbor Hills Mom-Mobiles—she flicked a harder look at her daughter. "Explain, please? You finished. You didn't finish. You didn't have to work on the fort?"

"We almost finished," Vivi clarified carefully. "We came close—we're asking for an extension, so it won't matter that we aren't done. We just need to go to the library—*today*."

"She's right," Elijah said earnestly. "We learned something new about our"—he coughed—"topic."

"Saturday night," Vivi added.

Quinn adopted teen lingo. "The internet is *a thing*, right?" She narrowed her stare on Vivi. She wanted to trust Vivi. Lord, she *needed* to trust Vivi. But right now, she could distinguish her unreasonable, ongoing anxieties from the chance that whatever these two were up to was something to be *reasonably* anxious about. "Couldn't you just Google it?"

Vivi let out a heavy sigh. "Mom, it's fine. I'll ask Belinger for an extension. We can show him what we *have* done then hit the library after school." Her expression turned funny. "Don't you *want* us to use the library? Isn't that, like, a *good* thing?"

Quinn caved and the line of cars rotated forward. Like passengers on a disappointing theme park ride, the two teenagers popped themselves out and gave her a half-hearted wave before hitching their backpacks and heading into the building.

The library.

Quinn's stomach churned at the thought. All those pre-touched books. The liberty of it—anyone at all breezing in and out, using the bathrooms and sharing the air and *enjoying* themselves for free in one big cavern.

Still, cramped though it made her stomach, she'd pick them up at the *library*. After school.

Heck, maybe Quinn would even turn up early and check the place out. Exposure therapy, right? Wasn't that what this whole adventure-to-a-new-town thing was about? Beating back her urges with a broom and clearing a new path?

Yes.

But first, the office.

First, her meeting with Forrest.

# CHAPTER 6—BEVERLY

Beverly Castle was set to meet Forrest Jericho at ten o'clock Monday morning. She had spent all of Saturday night and Sunday outlining her proposal for the new feature, the title of which was still ambiguous. Writing an advice column was out of her comfort zone, but wasn't everything these days?

That's what happened when you lost your world. You lost your comfort, too.

So, turning from fluff pieces and even the headier investigative pieces to Dear Abby was just another new thing. Something else to get to and to get through. But maybe it was one that would do her good. After all, nothing else had worked. Not the pills. Not the therapy. Not sleeping through the day. Maybe, if Beverly put herself out there, she could find a way to live again.

*Maybe.*

~

She arrived earlier than usual, at eight thirty, hoping to spend her time fine-tuning some points of interest over the outline for the first run.

A tagline would help, and she began there.

*Dear Abby meets Hedda Hopper.*

But how could that work? An advice write-in and a gossip column? Seemed improbable. Anyway, who would know about Hedda Hopper anymore? And in a small Michigan town, too. Hollywood gossip out of the 1930s was as far removed from small-town America as bad traffic.

Maybe the opening piece could invite submissions, like a call to audition. Or would she gather submissions from social media *first* and then do her writeups? When would they start the feature? This week? Next? Would it run daily? Weekly? Biweekly? This would depend on traffic.

She'd need Quinn's help with some of this. Quinn had her finger on the social pulse—how readers were interacting with the newspaper online. Who was the most interactive? Research showed that women over the age of forty were most active during the day. Younger audiences were active all times of day. A recent local poll indicated most Harbor Hills readers preferred to stick with one form of social media. A third of them used three or more. Only ten percent reported consistent engagement with any online news source and that was usually in Facebook comments on pieces that directly concerned them.

Would an old-fashioned advice column *concern* the locals?

Beverly didn't know.

She tapped away at her computer, working on a draft of an intro post. By the time she glanced at the clock, it was a quarter past ten and Forrest had yet to appear from his office. And Quinn had yet to appear at the office at all. Every so often, during the past hour, Beverly had heard noise crackle from behind his door. Likely, he was on a conference call. Every few Mondays, regional editors would join a call and rehash industry news, so to speak. They'd talk sponsorships and marketing, crossover stories, reporter swaps, and so on. Beverly had taken to hiding after said meetings, hoping to escape an assignment over to Birch Harbor. In small towns, you relied on the drama of other small towns more than anything else. Without their gossip, all you were left with were town council budget reports and traffic stops.

Truly.

At twenty past ten, Forrest's door cracked open.

Beverly frowned. It wasn't her cousin who appeared from within. "Quinn?"

Quinn's face was blank but flushed. She adjusted her sweater but not salaciously, in Beverly's estimation. "Oh," Quinn said simply. Gone were her usual ticks, the things that Beverly had recently started associating with her. The over-blinking and finger tapping and leg bouncing. She appeared, by all accounts, calm. Content?

But Forrest didn't. "Bev, hey." He came up behind Quinn and seemed awkward to be so near to her. Quinn picked up on this and excused herself, giving Beverly a short nod. "Lunch today, right? To talk social strategy?"

"Social strategy," Beverly echoed faintly. "Oh, yes. For the new feature. Noon," she confirmed, and with that, Quinn was off to her own desk.

Beverly cocked her head at her cousin and folded her arms. "What was that about?"

Hands in his pockets, he shrugged. "You know," he said, "adding social media to our proverbial plate has opened the door for a steady stream of drama."

"Oh?"

He waved her off. "It's fine. Nothing Quinn can't handle. New feature, right?" He began walking back into his office, and Beverly followed. "Dear Bev?"

"House with the Blue Front Door," she answered. "That's the working title."

"Doesn't sound much like an advice column. Or are we doing an advice column? Didn't you mention something about gossip? Like a Page Six thing, right?"

For being a small-town male and relatively young —in his forties—Forrest was well versed in his industry.

"I think advice. I mean, maybe somewhere in between could work, but I'd want to—"

"Like a venting space." He typed furiously on his computer then swiveled the monitor.

"Vent with Bev," she read from his screen. "Vent with Bev?" She gave him a look. Usually, Beverly played along at the office—that her cousin was her editor and boss. Her cousin, the dopey, curly-haired freckle face who tagged along with his brothers and had a puppy-dog crush on her when they were too young to know about crushes and cousins and all that. Usually, Beverly could pretend Forrest was in charge.

But sometimes, she had to drop the act. "Forrest, no."

"No?" his voice weakened, and he sank back into his seat. All the strength from his meeting with Quinn apparently dissipated. "Okay, so, then...?"

"I don't like Dear Bev or Dear Beverly, either. It's a rip-off. I want it to be my own. And I'm no therapist, so I realize it can't actually be an advice column. But it's not a good idea to *only* stir up local crap. Not good for the paper *or* the readership."

"But the Blue Front Door thing—no one will get it."

"It's a metaphor."

"For what?" He looked genuinely interested.

She explained. "Blue is...blue is an emotional color, you know? It's got the sad symbolism, sure. The blues, right? But it's also the color they say to paint your bedroom walls if you want a serene environment. It's the color of the sky." She didn't use the word she wanted to. *Heaven*.

"It's the color of water, too." Forrest leaned forward. He was getting it.

The last reason she loved it so much was because Tom hated it so much. Blue was Beverly's rebellion. It really was. But now that she was working on forgiveness, she figured she'd keep that particular dig to herself. Beverly hoped it was possible to forgive someone and still nurture those little angers. Sometimes, that was as therapeutic as forgiveness, anyway. Tending to your wrath like an insignificant pet—maybe a goldfish or a lizard the kids found and confined to a terrarium. Just important enough to feed and water and check on. Nothing more.

Nothing less.

"But some people around town *know* yours is the house with the blue front door, right? Anyone in Crabtree Court, for starters."

"So?" Beverly answered. She felt tired all of a sudden. Like maybe this was a bad idea. Maybe she should quit the paper. And everything else, too.

Forrest lowered his voice, softened it, too. "Do you want that sort of attention? For people to know where you live and all?"

"It's not about me, Forrest. It's about...*life*." It felt silly and big and cheesy, but she meant it. Her new column had the potential to do all the things she'd wanted to do as a reporter. Expose truths. Learn about the world and the people in it. And write her way to some version of freedom. She gave her cousin a look. "Why are you questioning me on this?"

His eyes widened and he stuttered to reply. "Um, I...I'm *not*, Bev. I'm not questioning you. It's just—I feel like, it hasn't even been a year. And my mom was talking to your mom and—"

She rolled her eyes. Whenever Forrest mentioned their mothers talking, she felt like a kid again. Her aunt and her mother had had their fair share of conflicts. Namely, the bed-and-breakfast. Other things, too.

But Forrest was undeterred. "We're all worried about you, Bev. It's going to be hard, you know?"

"What's going to be hard? Starting a new column? Or starting one that matters?"

"Who says what you already write doesn't matter?" he shot back. He was regaining his momentum, and this irritated her.

"Teacher turnover at the high school? If it's gossip you want, well, you're already *assigning* me gossip."

"I didn't *assign* you that."

She let the point go as it was moot. "Covering the Harbor Hills Fourth of July events doesn't exactly inspire me, you know. Neither does Gladys Groundhog or any other fluff piece."

"Fluff is what small towns *have*," Forrest reminded her. "And it's *safer*, Bev."

Beverly shook her head and looked away, staring at a framed article on the wall behind him. Forrest's prize-winning piece on the only large-scale tragedy Harbor Hills had ever known. A macabre story: the grave robbings of the early naughts. Like something out of a one-hundred-year-old gothic novel, a nocturnal and morbid vandal was caught stripping the town's oldest burial sites of their gold and silver. Forrest's youthful perspective allowed for a compelling feature that made its way to Detroit, putting Michigan in the spotlight of the American news cycle.

"More happens here than meets the eye, I'd argue," Beverly said. "Remember Temperance Temper?" She thought about the cold case the two neighbor kids were fantasizing over, dredging it up like a modern-day Lizzie Borden—exciting and provocative. Probably, it was neither of those things.

"The Temper case belonged to Detroit and Birch Harbor. Not Harbor Hills. We're too sleepy for something like that."

"She had connections in town. Her family was known here." Why Beverly was defending the story as something bigger was beyond her. She agreed with Forrest. It wasn't.

He shrugged. "She didn't go missing here. She didn't even live here." With a sigh, Forrest returned to his computer. "But you're right. More *does* happen, and if you really are up to it, Bev, then it's yours for the taking. I say dig right in. You could start with the school, you know."

Beverly smirked. "I'm doing the new feature. And I'm calling it The House with the Blue Front Door. Come in. Kick your feet up. And *dish*."

## CHAPTER 7—ANNETTE

The Becketts were due at the Best house at two o'clock. This afternoon appointment gave everyone the morning to do last-minute tidying.

After a final walk-through of Apple Hill, the four-some would move over to Dogwood Drive and do the final walk-through there.

It was currently half past one, and Roman and Annette were on the back porch, where they had a swing to match the one on the front porch.

This was to be the very last time they'd sit on that porch together, in that swing. The Beckett house didn't have a swing.

Annette shifted and sighed. "The new house doesn't have a swing, you know."

Roman said, “We’ll get a new one. Costco probably has an end-of-season sale right now.”

But it wasn’t really the swing that Annette had been mourning over the course of the past thirty-six hours.

“Hi!” came a voice across the distance.

Annette squinted through the morning sun to the northwestern triangle of their yard. Elora’s bright face appeared at the corner where their properties kissed. “Hi!” Annette replied back, even more brightly. But her gaze flew to the opposite corner of her own yard. The wreckage was now gone, thanks to Roman stepping up to the plate at the final hour. Annette had had to beg him, even after he had laid into her about how she had *promised* Elijah would take care of it. Elijah had tried to, but the task had proven too big and the timing all wrong. *He has a research paper due*, she’d reminded Roman. This hadn’t come as a reminder, of course. It was news to him. And because she still didn’t know how to handle things, she couldn’t remind Roman that beneath a shallow layer of soil lay a skeleton, and how could Roman assign such a gruesome chore to their teenager? But there was one angle that could work. *You are the one who said we had to downsize. The one who gave up our office, remember?* Roman took Sunday morning to load up the wood and haul it away to a scrap shop that accepted drop-offs whenever.

But though the rubble was gone, the truth remained beneath that silty, churned-up soil and

Annette's prayers that she'd find a way *out* of this disaster.

Roman, none the wiser, now raised a hand and gave a kind wave. "Hello over there!"

"I'm on doggy-doo duty," Elora called back, beaming. She lifted her voice even higher. "That's what you're relegated to on moving day if you're pregnant."

Annette laughed politely, and Roman stood to walk over.

How she wanted to tug him down and hide. How she wanted something to happen to delay things.

Because if the Becketts knew what lurked in the corner of their new backyard, Annette feared they'd renege. And if they reneged, then where would the Bests go? Who'd cover their mortgage? How would they keep everything intact in Harbor Hills?

Well, they wouldn't. Their future was hanging on this property exchange. Without it, they'd be...well, they wouldn't be the Bests, she supposed.

The question was, initially, would decades-old remains really be enough to upset the deal?

Then again, that alone shouldn't change anything. Harbor Hills wasn't the first Michigan suburb to host yesteryear's backyard burial sites.

The real hang-up was a different question altogether—one posed by Elijah and Vivi on Saturday night. One that had come together when Annette had realized there was no marker. Nothing to indicate this was a case of a family putting a loved one to eternal rest six feet under.

The *real* question was: Who was buried in Annette's backyard?

And why?

## CHAPTER 8—ANNETTE

Back in the house, with the clock ticking its way closer to the key exchange, Annette wrung her hands and chewed her lip. Roman hummed contentedly as he leaned against the kitchen island, scrolling through his phone. Roman wasn't normally a phone person. He liked to work *with real people*, he'd often say.

"What time is it?" She asked this out of boredom and a need for his attention more than anything. Her phone sat on the kitchen island, in full view.

Roman didn't even look up. "One fifty-five."

She leaned back and glanced through the kitchen window, once framed with fresh herbs growing straight out of little terracotta pots. For looks, mainly. Usually, Annette just grabbed a little plastic package of organic herbs from the market. It was far easier than rationing her window garden.

That may have to change, however, and soon.

"Knock, *knock*!" trilled a pretty, young voice at the front door. The wooden door itself stood wide open, allowing for a cool autumn breeze to blow through the house and clear it of those pheromones from families past. This was a trick Annette and Roman always used with open houses.

Of course, this deal was signed, sealed, and delivered. So it was unnecessary that Annette air the place out for the Becketts.

Annette rolled her shoulders back, shaped her mouth into a winning smile, and called back, "Just a moment!"

Roman continued scrolling on his phone, either unaware that the big visitors had arrived or indifferent. Probably the latter. Annette forced herself to temper the huff that grew in her chest. They needed a united front.

Especially today.

"Roman," Annette hissed.

He didn't look up. She frowned in the direction of the door. "Roman!" This time louder.

He looked at her through a haze of phone-fog and pushed his glasses up his nose. "They're here?"

"I have to ask you something." Why she'd waited

until this very moment, Annette didn't know. But it hit her, and she went with it.

Roman put his phone down and offered a bewildered gape. "Okay."

His typical apathy cleared, making way for something not far from interest.

"When you and Elijah built the fort, did you *find* anything?" She winced at her own phrasing.

"Find anything? No?" He shrugged and picked his phone back up, pointing with it toward the door. "Are you going to let them in, or should I?"

She could feel a tight cord in her neck snap. "Ouch." Her hand flew to it, rubbing hard at the nerve. "No. I will."

Pushing away from the island, she had precisely five seconds to make a call. Five seconds to make a call that she'd had the past day and a half to mull over. It just so happened that the only way for Annette to finalize her decision was to be directly confronted with it.

Which, she now was.

"Elora, Tad!" she greeted, deceptively cheerful. "Come *in*. I'm *so* excited." She waved a hand into the house, indicating they start with the kitchen, where Roman had finally pocketed his phone and stood beaming like Roman Best, Realtor. "*We* are so excited," Annette added. "There's just...*one* little thing we need to talk about. Just a technicality."

Tad and Elora studied her. The toddler tugged at his mother's pant leg, a stretchy one to accommodate his two little siblings growing inside.

"Why don't you come in. Please. Come," Annette urged.

They followed, if reluctantly.

Roman, who was still and ever out of the loop, boomed a generous hello and plucked his keyring from the counter, ready to toss it to Tad. Horrified, Annette cut this gesture off by holding her hands up.

"Roman!" she trilled. "I wanted to talk to the Becketts about something. You know, *before* we do all this?" She circled a manicured finger, indicating the house and the walk-through, then gave her husband the eye. He clutched the keyring in his palm, and his face fell.

"Oh. Um. Sure?" He turned awkward and sheepish, but the undercurrent of his charm persisted. Rosy cheeks beneath the thin, silver frames of his glasses. Bright white teeth gleaming through parted lips. If she weren't so stressed, Annette might forgive all their troubles right now and jump his bones.

Swallowing, Annette steadied her voice and leveled her chin. She didn't avoid confrontation under normal circumstances. She'd been the mom to stomp into a principal's office at the slightest suggestion of bullying—and not just against Elijah. Annette took it as her serious duty to stand up for any child. Any *person*.

Often with their real estate deals, Annette didn't

shy away from giving a client a little extra push in the direction of closing.

But then, if she were always so successful with her confrontations, why were they in this particular position? Standing at their own kitchen island—which was soon to be *not* theirs—staring at a young, far less ambitious and far more encumbered couple. A couple who would take the place of the Bests on Apple Hill Lane because Roman and Annette Best were, simply put, *not* the best. Not at their business, at least.

And this very deal, this very personal, very critical deal, could go up in smoke if Annette didn't play her cards exactly right.

"We've already signed the disclosure," Annette said, choosing her words with precision. There had been other options. She could have disposed of the skeleton—but for her Christian faith. She could have called the police who could then be the ones to break the news to the Becketts. She could have done any number of things to avoid this moment.

But she hadn't. She'd done nothing more than swear two teenagers to silence on the hope that the three of them, together, could simply *keep a secret.*

"Right," Tad agreed. "We signed our disclosure, too."

Elora looked at Annette hard, her head cocked to the side, following the line of her arm that disappeared into the toddler's grasp. "Did something *come up*?" she said by way of accusation.

Suddenly, Annette realized how little she knew about these people. They had been backyard neighbors. Nothing more. Silently cursing herself for not turning her busybody ways on the Becketts, Annette tried to interpret the younger woman's tone and response. Maybe this was a source of delight for young Elora? Maybe she liked excitement and drama?

She was pregnant with twins. She had enough excitement.

"Nothing related to the house," Annette answered. Roman raised an eyebrow at her. "It's to do with the backyard."

Roman made an *ahh* sound and nodded his head like he *remembered*. "The fort," he said.

Annette started to shake her head. *No, not the fort, silly husband.*

But Tad hefted up the little child pointedly. "If you didn't get a chance to take it down, I can."

"Oh, it's down," Annette chirped.

"Then what is it?" Elora asked darkly. Her eyes flashed, endearing her to Annette. This woman wanted deets. She *needed* deets. And not necessarily because those deets had a single thing to do with Elora.

Annette liked her.

And when Annette liked a person, she suffered

from incurable word vomit. "There's a grave in our backyard."

~

AFTER THE BIG REVEAL, Annette and Roman hung back on the porch with the little boy while Tad and Elora picked their way across the yard toward the clumpy soil in the far corner. If you squinted, you could see dusty ivory peeking up like a miniature, broken picket fence as Tad dug around with his toe.

Annette played a distracted game of patty-cake with the kid.

Roman whispered too loudly. "Why didn't you... bury it back down better? Or throw it away?"

"Throw it away?" Annette snapped. "So that this poor person winds up in the county landfill? Only to be discovered by someone who calls the cops, and a forensic team shows up, and they find our DNA on the bones and *boom*. We're in prison for a murder we didn't commit!"

Roman blinked back at her, his mouth partially agape. "Wow," he murmured. "That's an impressive leap."

She let out a sigh. "Roman, throw it away? Are you *serious*?"

"No," he snorted, "but why didn't you tell *me* first,

Annie? I mean...to blurt it out like that in front of them. Why?"

Annette wasn't sure. Why *was* she being so tight-lipped only to reveal it at the worst possible moment?

"I don't know, Roman," Annette muttered.

"Then again, these types of things are *everywhere* up here, Annie. Sheesh, you know that property on Pine Tree Place we sold a few weeks ago?" She nodded, annoyed. He went on. "A week after closing, the buyers sent me a few pictures. They had the backyard landscaped, and they found two markers at the far back of the property, where it butts up to the forest."

"You mean like what's out back of Quinn's house?" Annette referred to a vague memory she had of some old graves from ages ago. She was fairly certain some of them belonged to the original Carlsons. Not Carl Carlson, though. He'd been cremated and collected by a distant relative, according to Annette's source at the county mortuary.

But she was even more certain that what lurked in their backyard was no such old-timey tradition.

Roman scratched his head. "Old graves on the Carlson property?"

Annette rolled her eyes. Of course he wouldn't remember that, and of course he'd call it the Carlson property even months after Quinn Whittle had purchased it. She'd bet he'd conjure up the memory of the Pine Tree discovery forty years from now, but ask him what their anniversary was and he'd give his own mother's birthday.

The couple made their way back to the porch, and their little one ran to his mother, who reached down and grabbed his hand.

A dark expression hung over Tad's face.

A different expression lit up Elora's.

"What are you thinking?" Annette ventured to ask.

The two looked at each other; an unspoken exchange crossed between them. Something akin to affection and depth and warmth. Annette smirked. *Just give it a decade or two*, she wanted to say. *Your bond will soften.* She swallowed the harsh thought.

"You know, Roman makes a good point," Annette added, quelling the desperation in her voice. Roman looked surprised to hear such praise, but Annette tried to act casually. "These types of things are everywhere. It's surely just an old ancestor. Probably a Carlson. The original Carlsons developed this entire street, you know." Annette pressed her lips together.

Tad cleared his throat loudly, pushed his hands down into his pockets, and rocked back on his heels as if to allow his wife to answer.

And she did. "I doubt it." One hand gripped her son's and the other pressed against the underside of her extended belly. Laughter rippled through Elora's lips. "That's not a real grave. A real grave, well, you'd never have found bones."

"It *is* a grave," Annette shot back, sneering at the girl-woman. "What do you call a buried skeleton?"

Elora smirked. "Well, in this particular case, I'd call it a scandal."

## CHAPTER 9—JUDE

"Mrs. Banks?" A sharp rap cracked on Jude's wooden classroom door.

It was Wednesday afternoon. School was out, and Jude was anxious to get home and unwind from a long day of teaching. Her head snapped up at the sound, and she couldn't help but correct the intruder. "It's Miz."

"Oh, sorry." Mr. Ruthenberg, the principal, appeared in the doorway, his brows kinked up high on his forehead. It never ceased to amaze Jude how the Miss-Miz-Missus label confounded some people. Particularly men. It was surely a man's idea in the first place, no doubt.

"Have you seen this?" He moved aside and pulled a trifold presentation board into view, opening it to reveal three neat columns of images and information.

Old-fashioned for a modern high school student presentation. Almost all curricula had turned digital since the last time Jude had been in a classroom. Now it was PowerPoint this, online quiz that.

Had she seen a trifold project for someone else's class? "No," Jude answered blankly, standing from her chair as he moved deeper into her room.

She circled around her desk and joined him halfway to the door. The title of the project read, "What Happened to Temperance Temper?" Across the panes of cardboard were pasted three dim, photocopier-quality images.

The two flanking photos revealed groups of people. The one on the far left appeared to be a family portrait. Perhaps taken some time in the fifties. The one on the far right was either a school or company portrait. Over a dozen women in matching uniforms, squinting in the sunlight.

The largest photo, center, bore a neatly styled woman, simple in her beauty. She smiled tentatively at something off in the distance of her black-and-white world. Something the camera hadn't captured. Logic would have it that this happy-looking woman was none other than Temperance herself, of the Temper family. That missing woman with some loose tie to Harbor Hills.

Before Jude could read the students' research on their topic, Mr. Ruthenberg spoke. "Elijah Best and

Viviana Fiorillo turned it in to Mr. Belinger today. It's...*impressive*." His voice fell an octave over the last word.

Jude gave the project a dutiful look. It was impeccably organized and crafted. The use of white space symmetrical and pleasing to the eye. "Impressive, indeed," Jude agreed. But she wasn't sure why he'd brought it to her.

"I figured you might be interested in it," he said, flipping the board to its backside, where a printed page was taped. On the page, a short list of references, the students' works cited.

"Oh? Why?" she asked. "Are you worried they plagiarized or something?" She tried for an easy laugh, but it came out short and choking.

"It's not that, no," he answered. "Belinger dropped it off to go in the exemplar case in the front hallway. I happened to peruse it, and it just...well, I wanted to come to you, because they listed Beverly Castle as a source."

Jude stiffened. "Beverly?"

"Exactly," he agreed, although Jude was certain he didn't know *what*, exactly, he was agreeing with. In fact, she wasn't sure what his angle was at all. He explained. "Belinger tells me there's a follow-up assignment to the research presentation itself. The students are to take their piece to the town hall as a way to encourage community engagement in the school. I loved the idea when he originally pitched it to me. He said they could write in to the newspaper or speak at a town council meeting. They could even host an event if they were very ambitious." He chuckled nervously and fidgeted with the board awkwardly.

Jude frowned. "Okay?"

"Well, I'm just...*worried*," Mr. Ruthenberg said, his voice low. "About Bev's involvement."

"What do you mean her 'involvement'?" Jude asked, now ravenously curious.

"See?" He held the board up, and Jude devoured the information, beginning with the timeline that spanned the middle.

*Born in Birch Harbor November 1920. Left town to pursue higher education at the Detroit School for Women in Nursing, 1938. Graduated, 1942. Took up position with Bucklin Township Institutional Hospital, 1942. Hospital dissolved, 1975. Temper family formally requested missing persons investigation open, 1995.*

"This is all public record," Jude spoke of the biographical facts. "It has nothing to do with Beverly. Or even her article."

"The timeline, you're right. But they dug into her article and beyond." He stopped and gave her a funny look. "Have you read Bev's series?"

"Series?" Jude shook her head. "I thought she'd written just the one article." Jude hadn't even read that one. It was, quite literally, old news, after all. She hadn't even been around at the time the piece had come out, and from all she could tell, it hadn't made much of a splash. Why else would Beverly have continued to flounder in little local pieces? Had the article been a smashing hit—or a big piece of the puzzle that was Temperance Temper—surely Beverly would have been launched into a bigger publication than the little *Harbor Herald*.

"She had a three-article series. It was"—he cleared his throat and wiggled his eyebrows—"provocative."

"Provocative? How so?" She glanced at the clock on the wall. It was almost four, and Jude was in growing danger of starting her evening routine late. She felt itchy and sweaty.

He shrugged. "The first one was just the facts. The latter two...well...she tossed up some accusations about locals. There was a teacher who taught here, you see, and Bev was absolutely convinced this woman was involved. Bev came around the school and hounded the principal at the time. It wasn't me. I was just starting out teaching. Math. I saw her come in, though. Beverly, I mean. I saw her come in and hound people, and—"

"And what?" Jude pressed.

"It didn't go anywhere. Well, in terms of her investigation. But the community sort of shot back at her. They thought Bev was turning on her own people. Making the disappearance a witch hunt, even though

Temperance wasn't *from* here. She was a Birch Harbor girl. Why should a Hills woman protect a Harbor woman? That sort of BS." He shook his head.

"So? I mean so *what* if Temperance was from Birch Harbor?"

"Let's just say that if Harbor Hills is the House of Montague, then Birch Harbor is the House of Capulet. I bet you already have a sense of that, having worked at St. Mary's, right?"

"What do you mean?" Jude found herself hungry for any scrap of information Darry might provide. And provide, he did.

"The rivalry. Among teenagers it's especially bad. Football rivals. Volleyball. Heck, even our chess teams hate one another." He laughed.

She swallowed. "Of what did Beverly accuse locals?"

Mr. Ruthenberg tapped his finger on the bottom-center box, a pristinely trimmed square set against a red border. "That's why I'm worried. Viviana and Elijah have picked up right where Bev left off over twenty years ago. But they added a twist. Look."

Jude focused on the typewritten, so-titled Thesis and read under her breath. "'In 1995, Temperance Temper was on her way home to Birch Harbor from Detroit when she met with tragedy. Temper was killed in the then-fledgling town of Harbor Hills, Michigan. The killer, who may or may not be alive still today, buried her body somewhere in town. Known suspects from the time of her disappearance include three prominent local families.'"

Her gut clenched as the words rolled like marbles down her gullet, clacking together hard at the bottom of her stomach.

Beneath the thesis were three all-too-familiar surnames.

Carlson.

Gillespie.

And Jericho.

## CHAPTER 10—ANNETTE

A *scandal.*

The words rang like a death knell from Monday to Tuesday all the way to Friday, carrying Annette sleeplessly through the week. She'd expected it to go differently. She'd expected the Becketts to back out. She'd expected high drama.

Instead, everything had gone exactly according to plan. For some reason, this depressed Annette, even though she had very little reason to be depressed.

After all, Elijah had Homecoming the next day. Homecoming! Annette *lived* for Homecoming.

But Homecoming currently felt like the very least of her worries—or celebrations, as the case may be.

On Monday, Annette, Roman, Tad, and Elora had agreed that the skeleton was a problem. A problem big enough to affect the property exchange, Roman pointed out. As such, they came to an agreement.

They would call the police.

Roman, being the face-to-face kinda guy that he was, preferred for everyone to go into the station all together, as one happy group. Maybe he could even sweet-talk them into getting the mess sorted out by end of business Monday. Annette tended to agree. She'd have a clearer sense of what this meant for the real estate deal, anyway.

Tad had a different idea of how to proceed toward law enforcement, however. "I'll handle it," he had said. "I have a brother on the force."

"What force?" Roman had shot back derisively.

Tad replied, "County Sheriff's Office."

"This is a town matter. I'll just take it into the police station."

Annette grew tense. "If Tad has a brother on the *force*," she chimed in, "maybe that would be the fastest avenue to solve this." She tapped the ball of her foot on the floor, flicking a nervous gaze around the house. She was supposed to be out of there by then. In the cute, red cottage she'd worked up in her mind's eye as her own.

She caught Elora's stare. The woman looked too excited. Too impatient. Annette couldn't figure out if she trusted her. "I mean, what could be the harm in us moving in now, anyway? Does it matter? It's not illegal.

I mean...none of *us* is responsible for the skeleton, right?" She laughed, and Annette couldn't help but warm to her. Elora was a tough cookie, no doubt. But... to move in even under *these* circumstances? Surprising, indeed.

Preferring, for the moment, to be as agreeable as possible, Annette answered quickly. "Elora's right. It may be a *scandal*"—she drew out the word provocatively—"but it's not *our* scandal." Annette grabbed Roman's arm. "Right, honey?"

To Roman's credit, he returned a kind smile. "True." He looked at Tad. "We're comfortable with whatever you're comfortable with. If you want to call your brother, that's great. Or I'm happy to walk it down to the station here in town."

"I'll call. It'll be *fine*." Tad wrapped an arm around his wife.

After the surprisingly simple conversation, Annette and Roman had been further shocked to hear Tad and Elora express that they were just as happy to move in right then. On the spot. Skeleton and all.

That was Monday.

Now it was Friday, and Annette, Roman, and Elijah were tentatively unpacking themselves in their new home. Escrow had closed. The deal was done. Not even a dead body could have undone it. In a way, Annette felt like a failure to some degree. While the deal had gone through for now, it was only a matter of time before an investigation hatched open and she and Roman were implicated in the mess, somehow. Dread had tainted each day of the week.

And even with the plan in place, Annette had felt no closure after the discovery and revelation. Not only that, but it wasn't her own secret either. And when more than one person held a secret, was it really even a secret?

She had been waiting for the other shoe to drop on this very point when Elijah burst through the door after school on Friday.

"We turned it in."

"Turned what in?" Annette had just ended a phone call with a flakey new client—someone browsing the area. It was the first new lead in over a week, and she and Roman were taking anyone they could get. Especially after they learned that Lake Realty Executives had opened an ancillary office in Best on the Block's former space. Best on the Block was sinking fast, and their competition was seeing to it that they drowned.

"Vivi and I turned in our research project," Elijah replied.

Annette looked beyond her son. She was so used to him turning up with Vivi at his side that she now felt surprised. "Where *is* Vivi?"

"Getting her nails done for the dance."

Annette gave a little clap. "Oh, how *fun*." She had desperately wanted a daughter. When, after Elijah, she couldn't get pregnant again, she'd begged Roman to let her adopt a little girl. *From whom?* Roman had grunted. At the time, she'd have taken a baby from wherever, but then Elijah had started kindergarten and Annette reclaimed some of her social life and the idea of a new baby—or anything different—turned stale. The dream died. Or maybe she realized subconsciously that she'd been living the dream all along. That's exactly how it felt when Roman announced they were closing out their business front and slipping into financial straits. It felt like she'd been living the dream all along. She just hadn't given it much attention.

Shameful.

"So..." She drew out the word. "What did your teacher say?"

"About the project?" Elijah snapped a banana from its bunch and hunkered down at the kitchen bar. It was a narrow butcher block insert. Metal frame on wheels that could lock. Even if Annette wanted to dig her barstools out of the basement where they'd been temporarily stored, it was useless. Her new kitchen was much too small for added seating.

And that was okay.

Elijah leaned heavily on the oak top. "He seemed impressed." Elijah swallowed the banana in three big bites.

"So, that's it, then?" Annette asked. "Project submitted. Mystery solved?"

"Well, we didn't even solve the mystery. Our thesis was watered down, but that's what Vivi wanted."

"What do you mean?"

"I mean all we did was suggest a very big, very rough theory. You know"—his voice sank into that of a radio show host—"one of three families could be to blame. Stay tuned to find out who the culprit is."

"Are you going to dig deeper, so to speak?"

"What? You mean go looking for Temperance?" He shrugged and plopped the banana peel into a temporary trash can made from a paper grocery sack. "Vivi wants to. She thinks Belinger would give us extra credit or something."

"What about you?" Annette eyed him. "Do you think what happened in our backyard impacted this little report of yours?"

He rolled his eyes. "Get real. That thing is old. Way too old to be our girl," he said like a detective, and Annette had to chuckle.

"Whatever is in the yard is old news. I agree." She meant every word. "But it's funny, right?"

"By funny, do you mean coincidental?"

Her son was too smart for his own good. Again, Annette laughed. "Yeah, I guess I do. Woman goes missing. Body turns up."

"It's a little too perfect," Elijah allowed. "Anyway, I think both questions are dead ends. Like cold cases or something. Remember what Kayla used to say?"

Annette did not, and her blank stare suggested as much to Elijah.

"When I got wigged about a grade or a weird pain in my leg. Remember?"

This, Annette *did* remember. It still happened. Elijah was a hypochondriac with a capital *H*, and Kayla Castle had often been the one person in the world who could bring him down from near hysterics. "She assured you," Annette said.

"She said, 'Common things are common.'" His eyes turned a bit misty, but he wiped any emotion quickly away.

Annette's stomach twisted up over Kayla. "Common things are common," she repeated. "Sounds wise. But I guess I'm too dumb to get it."

"It means that ninety-nine percent of the time, a headache is just a headache. Not a brain tumor. And ninety-nine percent of the time, a kid who gets straight As is going to keep getting straight As."

"Common things are common," Annette echoed once more.

Elijah poured himself a glass of milk, downed it, and wiped his lips with the back of his hand. "Ninety-nine percent of the time, cold cases stay cold. Missing people don't turn up. And old skeletons in your backyard are just hillbilly graves."

Annette wanted to add something more, but Elijah

left the kitchen for his bedroom. Moody and angry and edgy all over again.

But what she wanted to say was that ninety-nine percent of the time, teenagers don't die in car crashes.

Ninety-nine percent of the time, everything turns out just *fine.*

## CHAPTER 11—ANNETTE

Annette pushed her fingers through her brunette hair, tugging the ends and measuring them with her eye. Time for a trim. Too bad Roman had tied the purse strings of late.

Bored and irritable, she went to the front door. The first two nights they were there in the little red cottage house, she hadn't had a chance to take a view from the front porch.

On Apple Hill Lane, she and Roman had swung on the front porch and back porch to a sideview of the sunrise and sunset.

Here on Dogwood, the front porch offered a striking panorama of the sinking Michigan sun. It nearly took her breath away. If only there were a swing or a hammock or even a little wicker chair to fall into. It was probably too chilly, anyway.

Annette stared off at the blurring lines of the horizon for a moment longer until her gaze fell to the little cobblestone walk that wove toward the street. How they'd all missed it was beyond her—Roman was normally compulsive about his morning funnies. But there it was, lying in the dew-damp grass to the side of the path. The *Harbor Herald*.

She strode out, bent with some effort—time to get back to morning walks—and scooped up the plastic-wrapped newspaper. Then, with one last look at the falling evening, Annette turned and went into her new house.

The house around the corner on Dogwood Drive. Not yet her home. Maybe it never would be, depending on what happened with the Becketts and the body on Apple Hill Lane.

~

"Can you set the table? Dad'll be here any minute."

"Where does he go, anyway? It's not like you guys have an office anymore."

Elijah had rejoined Annette just as soon as supper started wafting about the house. He leaned onto the little island, his phone glowing against his face while Annette worked on boiling water for sweet tea.

For a chilly autumn evening such as this, and with little more than the very, very basics to work with,

Annette had whipped together a simple roast in the crockpot. That morning, she'd thrown in three pounds of beef, added baby carrots and quartered potatoes, sprinkled Lawry's all over it, popped the lid on, and patted herself on the back. Annette wasn't a bad cook, but it had rarely been her priority in life. So, to pull something so down-home together under the current circumstances was nothing short of a gift. A gift for Elijah and for Roman. And maybe for herself, too.

Elijah was never this snarky. *Or* chatty. Something was up. Sighing, she tried her best to stay above his level. "He took around some fliers."

"Fliers?" Elijah looked horrified but dutifully reached for a stack of paper plates. "What do you mean?"

Roman's voice boomed from the front door, perfectly on cue. "I'm home!"

"We're in here!" she said, even though it was useless. Roman could see them plain as day. The front door gave way to the living room and kitchen—an open-space cabin-y design. But she was used to saying things like "We're in here" and "I'll be down in a minute," and old habits die hard. "How'd it go?"

"I finished Crabtree Court and the school neighborhood. I'm thinking of doing a little canvassing of Main Street tomorrow."

"What do you mean canvassing? What fliers?" Elijah asked again.

Roman held up a stack of handouts. "Hometown advertising. That's what it's all about, son. Reaching the people where they are. Lake Realty Executives can roll out billboards and social media ads all they want, but when it comes to buying a home, people want to *trust* the person who represents them."

Elijah hid any cringing by turning to deal the plates onto the table, one of very few pieces of furniture they'd set up. With so little work of late, Roman had offered to spend all Tuesday and Wednesday unpacking and putting the house together, as he called it. Annette had told him not to worry about it. What was the *rush*?

~

AFTER A QUIET DINNER, the three Bests sat with elbows propped on the table. Their clean plates had Annette beaming. She was even inspired to poke around at something close to normal conversation. "Ro," she began, swallowing the last of her after-supper coffee, a tradition carried down from Bertie and the B&B.

"Mm?" He sipped at his own cup.

"Elijah has Homecoming tomorrow. Think you can take him to get the corsage?"

Roman perked up at this. Homecoming, or any formal social event, was very much in Roman's wheelhouse. "Sure, *sure*. Have you ordered one yet? You've got to order ahead. What is Vivi wearing? Are you going with her?"

Annette inwardly beamed at Roman's surprising knowledge of the subtle romantic dynamics. To anyone else, Elijah and Vivi's advancing courtship was obvious. To Roman, Annette wasn't sure. She was glad to see he hadn't totally checked out. There was hope, yet.

Elijah nodded, but he didn't meet their gazes. "I guess."

Annette reared back. "What? You *are* going with Vivi. What do you mean?"

"She's bringing other girls, and they're bringing their friends. Guys I don't know. Football players."

"Nothing wrong with football players," Roman cracked. Roman was the opposite of America's dad. Never much for playing football, he appreciated the Superbowl only for the networking opportunities. Otherwise, he fully supported Elijah's interests in anything, sports or not.

"I know, it's just—you know. I don't know them."

"You'll have fun. Good to expand your horizons, E." Roman returned to his coffee like it needed immediate attention.

"Mom," Elijah said, crossing his arms and giving her a hard look. Elijah was rarely one to start a new topic, much less interrupt an ongoing one.

Annette braced herself, one hand pressing down

on the dark maple-wood top, the other clenching the handle of her teacup. It had never felt more delicate than in that moment, almost as if Annette had sensed what Elijah was about to ask. Like he was going to shatter something very tenuous.

"What's the word with the body?"

Annette forced her teacup to her lips, taking a slow, slurping sip as her gaze darted to Roman. His aloofness had returned, and he was fiddling with his Apple Watch.

"Elijah." She clicked her tongue and again looked at Roman, willing him to intervene. "You put it so crassly."

"We can't just pretend it didn't happen. Vivi is champing at the bit to tell her friends."

"It's not our news to share anymore." Annette meant this. "Right, Roman?"

Roman glanced up, but nothing more than befuddlement filled his face.

"Oh, for goodness' sake, *Roman*. You care about Homecoming but not the very thing that could undo our property exchange?" She wanted to cackle but suppressed it in favor of a sharp shake of her head.

"Undo our property exchange?" Roman frowned. "It's signed and over. We live here now, Annie. The Becketts live in our house." He wiped his hands and held them up. *See?* he said wordlessly. *No big deal!*

She silently seethed, forcing herself to take a series

of slow breaths. Regardless of what Roman thought about the exchange, he was right about one thing. Ultimately, it *was* no big deal. She said this aloud to their son.

"So, it's not a secret, then? I can give her permission?"

"Why does Vivi *need* to tell her friends? It's not a secret, but…it's a private matter." Annette clenched her teeth together. There really was no point in Elijah running with the news. Not *now*.

Or *was* there?

"Gossip in high school is currency. Vivi really wants girlfriends. She's getting sick of me or something. But no one trusts her. She's like this weird new kid with a past. The running away thing got around school, and people are calling her names." Elijah looked pained to relay this information.

"Names?" Annette set down her tea. "Mean names?"

"Are names ever nice?" Elijah sighed and ran his hands down his face. "Things are just…*weird* right now. I don't know. It's like Vivi needs something to lock herself in to school. Fame or glory or something. I don't know."

"I get that," Annette murmured. "The fame or glory thing. Social currency. What have you."

"So, she can tell?" He pulled his phone from his pocket, but Annette reached out, stilling him.

"No. Like I said. That all belongs to the Becketts now." Her argument was thinning faster than Roman's comb-over.

"But they aren't *doing* anything," Elijah said.

"How do you know?"

"Have you seen police over there? Vivi and I looked it up. If you find a dead body, there's always an investigation."

Annette frowned. "Maybe police came by while you were at school."

"Oh, come on, Mom. As if you and your friends wouldn't know if a forensics unit were camping out on our street."

Annette pursed her lips. "It's not our street anymore." Her tone and words fell into the cracks of the life she was patching up. Even saying it out loud felt like a lie. Or, at the very least, a half-truth.

But it was neither.

For now, at least, it was the whole truth and nothing but the truth.

So help her, God.

~

IN BED, on top of her spare sheets and a throw blanket, Annette sat with her laptop open to their business calendar. She did this every Friday because they usually had a busy Saturday lineup. However, there were no showings, no closings, *nothing* booked for the next day. So, Annette simply stared at her blank calendar, reading and rereading the few obligations that lay before her. Elijah's Homecoming dinner and dance. And a phone call on Monday with the potential client.

Annette clicked over to their website, double-checking that everything was updated. Listings, what few they oversaw, looked fine. The MLS feed was accurate. Their brand blazed across the header. *Best on the Block Realty. Never settle for less.*

She snorted and closed the computer.

Roman was in the kitchen, where he'd connected the printer. He wanted to print extra fliers so they were ready for the next round. She had promised him she'd take over canvassing in the morning, as long as she could be home by noon to help Elijah get ready.

While the website seemed fine—better than fine, even—something about it rubbed Annette wrong. Something was missing. Or maybe...maybe it was the opposite issue? Too much crap?

Mentally stunted but wired, she eyed the newspaper she'd grabbed that afternoon. Roman had freed it from its plastic sleeve and read it after dinner. It now sat, neatly folded, in his spot. Shrugging to herself, she ignored the glow of her phone and instead grabbed the paper, thumbing through the different sections to the easy reading. Past politics. Past real news and onto the horoscopes, comics, crossword, weather, and TV guide.

She did about a quarter of the crossword. Mentally noted that her favorite show was airing its newest season the following week, devoured the comics, compared her horoscope against real-life recent events.

Still unsatisfied, she flipped to the back of the lifestyle section, where the classifieds rotted. At least, that's what Annette thought of old-fashioned print classifieds anymore. Who paid per line for a dead marketing source instead of uploading to the hottest social media marketplace? Not Annette.

Even so, that's just how bored and fidgety she was feeling. Bored and fidgety enough to read the classifieds, for goodness' sake.

Farm equipment, pets up for adoption, some well-loved sectionals. Then, there it was, taking up the entire bottom half of the section—a *Harbor Herald*–sponsored advertisement. A call for submissions.

*Got a secret? Something to confess?*

*Got a problem? Need advice?*

*Write in to our new multiplatform feature, and be the first to get the answers you need. Send submissions to The House with the Blue Front Door today!*

Annette reread the ad again and then a third time.

A smile curled up her face.

## CHAPTER 12—QUINN

It was Homecoming Saturday, and the week had been a blur. Cleaning and fretting and whispering prayers had dominated most of Quinn's waking hours. All that *plus* trying to corral Beverly into something feasible for the big debut feature. They'd already started farming submissions from their social media accounts and with a half-page ad in the print edition. It was a lot to handle.

In fact, it was getting to be that time of year when Quinn's anxieties and compulsions—her obsessions, too—got out of hand. From October to December 25, it just felt like one thing after another. And in the past two years, she'd struggled enough managing her own participation in the holidays. Now she'd be managing Vivi's high school events, too. And it all began with Homecoming.

Vivi's big research project was the first matter of business. It turned out the teacher decided to weight the assignment as a midterm, and this freaked Vivi out. Generally, she didn't show any hints of following in her mother's footsteps with the OCD thing. Vivi was confident and unfazed by common stressors. Sometimes wild. Sometimes troubled. Never OCD-y. But teachers and admin at Hills High had made a huge to-do about GPA and college scholarships and all the things that Quinn figured wouldn't appear on their radar until junior year. With only a 3.8 GPA transferring over from Birch Harbor, Vivi had realized she wasn't getting by on her smarts alone. She'd have to up her game. More honors courses. More AP courses. More As across the board.

So, when she and Elijah submitted their research project four days late, Vivi's attention tore away from Homecoming and settled over how and when Mr. Belinger would grade them.

Elijah, for his part, hadn't cared nearly as much. He considered their project to be *enough.*

The disconnect over how they did on the project had bubbled over into their Homecoming plans, too. This was the problem.

At the very last minute, Vivi decided to accept a group invite to join two other couples. Yes, she'd bring Elijah, but the whole thing was a clear message.

Vivi didn't need her new pseudo-boyfriend to get

by at Hills High. If he wanted to tag along, then *whatever.*

The whole change in plans meant that Quinn was now chewing aggressively on a hangnail in the corner of Main Event Hair and Nails. Occupying three of the four chairs were Vivi and two other girls who Quinn had met two hours earlier, when they appeared with their mothers at the salon, too. The two other moms knew each other, naturally, and knew the two stylists who were splitting their time across the three girls. It seemed like Vivi had burrowed her way into a pair of best friends, and Quinn was worried about this. Would she be the third wheel? What about her best friend, Mercy? Why hadn't Vivi tried to bring her over from Birch Harbor if she was feeling on the outs? Who were the girls' dates? Was Elijah comfortable sharing his night with an entire party of people?

It could be worse, of course. As they were arriving to Main Event, a string of five giggling teen girls unspooled from the shop, laughing and ignoring the incoming trio.

High school was hell.

Hair complete, beachy waves all around, even on Vivi's typically pin-straight locks. Next was makeup, and it looked to be getting heavier by the minute. Quinn didn't mind if Vivi wore heavy makeup. It was the one thing she'd appreciated about her own mother —the freedom of expression. No, she wasn't game for unusual piercings or tattoos. But a strip of pink hair dye or smudges of black eyeliner were okay by Quinn. None of that meant that any of *this* felt right, though.

The other two girls finished first, and their mothers commenced the gushing and fiddling. Vivi was nearly done, too, so Quinn sidled up to her. "You look gorgeous, honey," she cooed, picking an invisible piece of lint from the white button-down shirt Vivi wore. She'd change into her glittery dress at home with the other girls, who'd be coming over for the first time. *With* their mothers.

Vivi had accomplished this by bragging about their new house, Quinn was certain. However, wasn't it odd that they were so willing to overhaul their original plans and glom on to Viv? Quinn suspected there was more to it, and the fear of what that could be churned her stomach up like a bubbling hot spring.

Everyone's date was due to arrive by six, and it was all too much for Quinn, which was why she was so glad that Annette had agreed to take over. She was there now, setting up appetizers and drinks and light decorations. Just enough to spruce the place up and make Quinn feel that her foray into the small town wouldn't appear as rocky as it really had been. With Annette's help, Quinn and Vivi would be made to look good. Better than they were, maybe.

"Mom," Vivi whispered when the stylist drifted to a back room for a fresh tube of lip gloss.

"Yeah?" Quinn folded her arms over her chest and studied her daughter. Vivi was objectively beautiful. Dangerously so, even. She was the sort of teenager who could be plucked out of the real world and deposited into a fashion magazine or a TV show. It made for awkwardness at times, especially since she was the new girl. When Vivi was just a baby—a beautiful, bouncing thing—Quinn worried about fevers and milestones and nutrition. She worried about Matt being too absent. She worried she'd leave out a cleaning product and disaster would strike.

Now, though, she worried about other things. Things that seemed bigger. Really, they probably weren't. A mother's fears didn't grow bigger or shrink down smaller. They shape-shifted, mainly. Always the same level of threat.

"Can everyone sleep over after the dance?"

Quinn frowned. "Sleep *over*? At our house? That wasn't the plan, Viv. Wasn't Elijah going to take you to the movies after the dance?" The little theater at the top of Main Street was playing *Halloween*, and it was local tradition for the high school kids to go see a scary movie after the dance ended.

"I figured we could just watch the movie at home."

"You said *everyone*," Quinn pointed out, stealing a glance at the other two made-up girls. They were pretty, too. Not as pretty as Vivi.

"Well, the whole school is going to be at the

theater, so I figured it could be more chill to do something lower key. You know?"

*Chill.* Quinn blinked and chewed hard on her lower lip. Hard enough that she tasted blood. She licked it away and looked again at the others.

Vivi lowered her voice. "Mom, *please*? I mean our place is so huge, and we're getting ready there, anyway. I figured you'd appreciate us sticking close to home, right? I mean, it's safer than being out so late."

"But won't the whole school be at the theater? Safety in numbers." Quinn could feel it creeping back up. That same thing that had plagued her two years back when Vivi had given up and thrown in the towel on the whole mom-custody thing. The selfishness. She clenched her jaw and forced a smile. "What am I talking about? I'd love for you to bring them over after. I don't think the boys can stay the night, though—"

"Mom, everyone does it."

"Does what?"

One of the other mothers appeared on Vivi's left side. "Are you talking about the sleepover? Oh, Quinn, sure! You'll *be* there. It's *safe*."

"For the boys to stay the night?" Quinn started to shake her head. "I don't think that's—"

The second mother joined, too. "It's a small-town thing. If they aren't hanging out together at one of our houses, Lord knows what trouble they get up to in the woods."

The woods. *What happened to the movie theater?* Quinn swallowed. "Um, right. I guess I can just stay up and supervise," she said uneasily. It sounded exhausting, but Vivi's eyes were pleading, and there really was no choice. "Yeah, sure. That'll be fun." She pressed her lips into another smile, but inside she was screaming.

# CHAPTER 13—BEVERLY

Beverly spent Saturday morning at home combing through feature submissions. It was a tight deadline, from Monday through Friday. Still, she'd received just north of thirty, and this was a great surprise to her, because it sometimes felt like only thirty people lived in the whole of the town.

Of those thirty submissions, three earned a spot in the Sunday print debut, which she had to pull together by that very evening. If there happened to be more than three high-quality, highly engaging submissions, they'd roll over to the social media pieces.

By noon, her stomach growled loudly enough to spur her to action. With little to eat at home and excited to feel the pull of hunger—a rare event in the highs and lows of her days—she set off to the market.

Beverly never went to the local grocery store on a

Saturday. Inevitably, she'd bump into half a dozen people who *hadn't yet had a chance to offer condolences.* But she really was hungry, and it was Homecoming Saturday, so more likely than not, any of Kayla's friends or their families would be tied up with that. A trip to the store might just work.

As soon as she stepped through the whooshing automatic doors, warmth hit her face. That had been another effect of the ordeal. Beverly sometimes didn't have a gauge on the temperature. It'd be freezing out, and she'd be in a tank. It'd be sizzling out, and she'd be shivering beneath one of Tom's old pullovers. That was before she chucked all of his clothes, though.

Still, now, she met with the warmth readily, taking a breath and inhaling the smells of Northeastern Drugstore and Goods. She beelined to the deli counter, opting to first grab a sandwich and eat it in the little indoor café.

Thankfully, the attendant was an unfamiliar face, and they made her turkey on white without so much as making eye contact. Beverly filled a plastic cup with diet pop and headed for the three or so tables.

"Beverly!"

The voice came from behind, and her skin shriveled against her bones. A chill crested her spine, and her appetite began to slip.

At first, she pretended not to hear and simply took another step into the café.

"Bev!"

She squeezed her eyes shut and walked more quickly to the farthest corner table.

The voice was gone, and she was safe.

Swallowing before she even took a bite, Beverly willed her hunger to return. A sip of pop, and she took a tentative bite of the sandwich.

Then the voice returned. "I knew it was you. Hey."

Beverly looked up, her mouth full but her jaw locked.

When she saw him, relief washed over her, and she managed to work the bite of sandwich down her throat. She even spared a smile. "Darry."

~

AFTER THEY FINISHED THEIR SANDWICHES—BEVERLY ate every last bite—Darry wiped his hand on a napkin, balled it up, and asked, "Time to shop?"

She gave him a blank look for a moment. "Oh," she laughed. "Right. Because I'm at the store."

He nodded slowly but not in a mocking or patronizing way. In a way that meant they were sharing this joke. Her cloud of confusion was a silly, sweet thing. Maybe even *she* was a silly, sweet thing.

"Actually, I just came to grab a bite then get back to work. I might shop later, I guess." It occurred to her that she could do with some groceries. Coffee, namely.

Always coffee. She may even have a prescription refill lurking behind the drug counter.

"Work, huh? What's your latest story?" He dropped his voice. "Let me guess—you're going to take on that grave robbing thing from back in the day."

She shook her head and slurped the last of her pop. "Nope. It's a new thing. A weekly column." A frown knitted her brows. "I'm kind of...looking forward to it?" This came out as a question, but he understood her.

"That's great, Bev," Darry answered. "Are you writing it now?"

She pulled her laptop from her satchel. "First, I have to pick the submissions. It's sort of an advice column. Advice column meets gossip thing, I guess?" She felt herself flush. "It's weird. I know, it's—"

"Sounds like fun."

"Fun." She smirked. "Yeah. Anyway, we've got around thirty people with either problems or blather or tall tales. Some missed the mark entirely and sent in photos of their pets or grandkids." She shook her head lightheartedly.

"Sounds like what people *need* is somewhere to share about themselves."

"Yes, you're right." Beverly turned serious. "I think, ultimately, that's the goal. Everyone has a story they want to share. Or a connection they need to make. So, welcome to The House with the Blue Front Door." She beamed at him as her document populated. "Wanna hear the frontrunners?" she asked him easily, but in fact it was a big deal. Especially considering the frontrunners.

"By 'frontrunners,' do you mean the people with the biggest problems? Or the cutest pets?"

"Something like that." She tapped around on the keyboard. "I used two different general criteria to weed through the submissions. One being, is it highly relatable? And/*or* two, is it highly engaging?"

"Can people see themselves in the narrative? Or is it juicy?"

"Hah. *Juicy*. Yes. Something like that." She scanned the document in front of her, weighing whether to divulge the three pieces or not. Or maybe to divulge *some* but not others. "You sure you don't have anywhere to be? Aren't you chaperoning the Homecoming dance tonight?"

"That's hours away. I've got nothing but a bachelor's grocery list ahead of me. Spill."

She let out a playful sigh. "Okay. If you say so." And with that, Beverly read.

*Dear Blue Front Door,*

*Thanks for considering what I have to say. Years ago, Bertie Gillespie hosted a Christmas gala at the B&B up on*

*Main Street. Do you know why she stopped doing that? It was such great fun. Really kicked off the holiday spirits!*

*Blessings,*

*A Summer Resident Who Might Want to Be a Full-Timer*

BEVERLY GLANCED UP. "It's Mrs. Griggs. A parttime in Crabtree Court. She is the only 'summer resident' of Harbor Hills, I swear. And she *knows* I write for the *Herald*. She *knows* Bertie is my mom. Why not just ask me?"

Darry shrugged. "Sounds like she *is* asking you."

"She doesn't even come to town over wintertime. Hates the snow. Stays in Florida. Just like Shamaine, but much, much older."

"Maybe she'd come back if your mom put on that gala." Darry had a sheepish look, and Beverly just had to shake her head.

"You're right. I might just call Mrs. Griggs outright to answer this one."

"But isn't the point of this supposed to be a town-square sort of thing? You know, for people to open the conversation in a bigger way than by phone call? Maybe Mrs. Griggs is griping about the Christmas gala to lots of locals. Now is your chance to answer this question for her *and* for them. Right?"

He had a point.

Beverly marked the submission a hard maybe and read the next.

Dear House,

*My son is a student at Hills High. Long story short, he thinks a certain teacher plays favorites and treats the male students worse off. I've taken this issue up with the administration and the school board only to be pooh-poohed. There is no other teacher who offers the class my child needs. This matter could affect his GPA. What would you do? Thanks for considering.*

*Yours,*

*Upset Mother*

Darry rolled his eyes. "I bet I know who that is."

She held a finger to her lips. "It's anonymous. Don't say."

"Well, my advice to her is to *talk to the teacher*. Parents don't mind confronting the powers that be, but in the meantime, they throw a decent teacher under the bus."

"Are you sure it's not the teacher's fault? Maybe the teacher needs a talking to. Or a second talking to, as the case may be?"

Darry waved her off. "What's next?"

Beverly pursed her lips but moved to the last one. The best one.

*Dear Blue,*

*Can we call you "Blue"? I think my partner is having an affair. There. I said it. Or I guess I wrote it. How would you handle this? Or maybe you* have *handled this. Do you entrap them and expose them? Then what? Make it work? Leave? Kill them? Joking. Mostly. Oh, Blue. Help me. Please.*

*Yours,*

*A Neighbor in Need*

"A neighbor in need," Darry reverberated. "Do you think she's a literal neighbor or just a neighbor in the sense that this is meant to be a neighborly type of column?"

Beverly sighed. "I don't know. I mean, if she were an Apple Hillbilly, I'd know. I mean, I think I'd know. Quinn is divorced. Jude is divorced. Shamaine is entirely out of touch, even more so than Jude ever was. That leaves Annette, but Roman would never cheat."

"Whoever it was, they were careful with language. 'Them.' 'Partner.' Could have been a man who wrote in."

"Or even someone who's dating. Quinn and Forrest seem to be an item. I can't see her writing in, though."

"Well, like you said. It's anonymous."

"Right. We filter them through a form where they don't have to give a real name or real contact information." Beverly lowered the laptop screen. "Anyway, I'm not sure how to even answer that one. I think people would love to read it, and it'll stir up interest. But is it too far? I mean, could I get in trouble for libel or slander with this sort of thing?"

"I doubt it. Besides, you *do* know how to answer. Right?"

Beverly blinked.

Darry leaned across the table, one hand sliding closer to where hers rested on her wireless mouse. She grew hot. "Bev, if Tom were still alive, where would you two be now?"

She had zero interest in thinking about Tom when she was with Darry.

Maybe that was the answer. Maybe that was an answer all along. Another piece of the puzzle of forgiveness. Of moving on.

"We wouldn't have stayed together. I'd have left."

"And why not?" he pressed gently.

She blinked again then focused her gaze on Darry. "Because I never wanted to save our marriage to begin with. But I can't tell her to leave him."

"You don't tell her to leave him. You ask her if she loves him."

Beverly's gut clenched. "What if she loves him, but

he doesn't love her? Or vice versa if this is a man writing in?"

"Well, she or he will have to explore that, too."

Beverly nodded, equally saddened and motivated. "What are you doing for breakfast tomorrow?"

His eyebrows shot up, and he retracted his hand a few inches. "Breakfast? Tomorrow?"

She nodded and moved to pack up her laptop. "I think I'm going to do my shopping now. Maybe I'll pick up some Texas toast for cinnamon French toast. Do you like French toast?"

"Are you kidding?" He grinned. "I love it."

## CHAPTER 14—JUDE

After canceling on Dean the previous weekend, he'd suggested they do something more casual.

Because she wasn't entirely rude, Jude had agreed to grab coffee and go for a walk down Main Sunday morning. *After* Mass, of course. One could imagine Jude's surprise, however, when she arrived for the eight o'clock service at St. Joseph's to find none other than Dean Jericho chatting with the deacon, who was greeting parishioners as they moved past the holy water.

"Hey, Jude," Dean said simply. She knew he wasn't cracking a joke because he wasn't really smiling. More than anything, confusion spread over his face. "You come here?"

"To St. Joe's?" She pressed a hand against her chest.

"Well, yes. Usually eleven o'clock service." This was a stretch. Jude had only just begun attending Mass again. It had never in a million years occurred to her that she'd find her handyman there, and she wasn't sure how she felt about it. For the greater part of Jude's life, her faith had been hers alone, to be shared with God the Father, Son, and Holy Spirit. No one else. Not even *Gene*. Sure, her ex had attended Mass with Jude, but only because it was a social event. A tradition. Not because he was deeply religious or even spiritual.

"I'm more of a Saturday evening sort of guy myself." Dean grinned and followed her as she moved toward her favorite pew, the third from the front on the right hand side.

Saturday Mass. *Go figure*. Jude genuflected. Dean did not.

*Go figure.*

Mass went about as expected. The only awkward moment being the offering of peace. Jude went in for the usual handshake, but Dean leaned in for a hug. The resulting exchange was a horrifying crunch of their right hands between their bodies. No embrace. Just the squeezing of church clothes against their hands.

After, Dean wondered aloud if they should just do the coffee and doughnuts in the family center rather than move over to Main Street. "We're here."

If it were Jude and a close friend, she'd have

suggested the same. But wasn't this meant to be a casual date? Didn't Dean care about appearing, well, *cheap*?

But the coffee and doughnuts may be exactly what she was comfortable with. "Sure," she replied, following him out of the parish hall.

~

THEY SETTLED TOGETHER at the emptiest folding table where two aluminum frame chairs sat coupled on the linoleum floor. Crumbs from the children's Sunday school class peppered their eating space, but before Jude had a chance, Dean swept them into one hand and marched them to a nearby trash can. He then brushed his palms together and down his jeans. Yes, jeans to church—*go figure*.

"Tell me about yourself," he said, forgoing any chat about weather or box office hits and glugging coffee down his throat.

She watched his Adam's apple bob before taking her own first sip and choosing which detail about herself she might like to share with him. There were precious, *precious* few.

Personal facts whirred through her mind. Well, let's see. She was divorced. An only child. Had a cat, and that cat was the thing gluing her to some semblance of a life. She liked routines. She wasn't much for travel, not anymore, these days. She was a reader.

"I'm a reader." She nibbled the edge of her cinnamon twist.

"As in *books*?" He frowned and eyed the inside of his paper cup.

Bristling, she answered, "Well, yes. What else is there to read?"

He reached for the newspaper that sat in shambles in the middle of the table, pulling out a skimpy section of the Sunday edition. "The paper. I read the paper every morning with my coffee."

"Fair enough," she muttered, her eyes catching on the front-page column. "Oh my." Jude covered her mouth with her hand.

"What?" Dean shook it out and spread the page for both of them to read.

"It's Beverly." Her eyes flew across the title and over three distinct questions, each with a paragraph's-long response, presumably from Beverly.

"Beverly Castle." Dean grunted. "Sure. Your neighbor. *My* cousin."

Jude didn't bother with a response. Instead, she craned her neck to read what the woman next door had to say. She felt a vicious need to digest every last word.

. . .

*Dear Summer Resident,*

*You're right. It used to be that Bertie's, in conjunction with Main Street and even some notable residences, would put forth a beautiful Christmas gala. It was quite a bit of work to coordinate, as you can imagine. For those reading who weren't around back then, Harbor Hills came together to put on a three-day holiday extravaganza, beginning with a home tour on day one. A light parade on day two. And, lastly, a big Christmas banquet at Bertie's B&B, which normally overflowed to the garden, where Bertie would erect heat lamps and chimineas to account for the cold December weather.*

*Frankly, the event got a little too big and the coordinators too few. Over time, it dwindled to nothing, and I agree with you, Summer. It's a shame that such a lovely tradition has died.*

*Although I, myself, am unable to organize a Christmas gala, I'm hoping that there are some readers who might feel inspired to take up the good fight once again. Bertie's was a bit too small. Maybe there's another location—or hostess—who might take on such a festive event.*

"I remember that," Dean commented, tapping a rough finger on Beverly's reply, indicating he'd finished at the same time as Jude.

"You do?" she asked. "You went?"

"Well, sure. Whole town did. Bertie's was way too

small, but Harbor Hills doesn't have much in the way of an event venue. Been an issue forever. I remember when my brother got married, they just did it in my folks' backyard."

"Summer wedding, I guess?"

He shook his head. "Fall. It was freezing as all get out. But you know, the best part of that gala thing wasn't even the dinner."

"What was it?" Jude asked, thirsty for this information, though she hadn't a clue why.

"It was just—well"—he scratched his head and shoved the last third of the glazed doughnut into his mouth and didn't bother to chew much before finishing his thought—"the coming together of the town, really. All the stuff they did. That tour and the lights. It sort of shaped us during the holidays. Heck, folks from all over would come to Main Street."

"I can't believe they don't do it anymore," she answered. "If it was that popular."

"For things like that to work, you need the right people in the right places. Guess we don't have that anymore."

Jude studied Dean. He wasn't sexy or dashing. He wasn't muscular or even all that tall. He seemed like a nice man. A simple man. A man who enjoyed his small town and didn't much mind if he never ever left. She set her doughnut down on the paper plate and frowned at him. "Maybe things will go back to the way they used to be."

But Dean grinned and shook his head. "Things never go back to the way they used to be. That's the beauty of life, after all."

She swallowed, intrigued.

*Things never go back to the way they used to be.*

Perhaps Jude, more than anyone, knew how true this was.

## CHAPTER 15—VIVI

Homecoming dance started out even more awkwardly than Vivi could have pictured. Logically, she knew that sparks weren't going to fly with Eli just because a throng of teenagers were grinding to heavy bass. He didn't have the moves that her old boyfriend did. Eli was stiff and uncomfortable, and that sort of repelled Vivi as the night throbbed on.

She ended up dancing with other guys—nameless ones—until her two new girlfriends spotted her and awkwardly dragged her back over to Eli, who, by then, was sulking in a chair next to a teacher.

Vivi crossed her arms and made a face, but it had little effect on her date.

"Ready to go?" he asked half-heartedly.

"The dance isn't over." She slid her gaze to the

teacher, whose eyes she felt. Vivi was used to feeling men's eyes. Women's, too. It wasn't her body, she knew. She was a little too skinny to attract stares for that. It was something else. Her overall look, someone had once told her. Like she was someone famous but they couldn't pin down exactly what movie she was in. Or what TV show. Or what YouTube channel.

The teacher didn't look away. Instead, he smiled at her then elbowed Eli. "Yeah, Elijah. The dance isn't over. Get back out there. Let's see some moves."

Vivi and Eli exchanged a look, and a smile broke out on each one's face. A secret mockery of the goobery male teacher.

Without answering him, Eli pushed up from his seat and grabbed Vivi's hand, lacing his fingers through it. "Let's go talk."

Titillated by his sudden show of force, Vivi let him pull her to a dark, hollow corner of the gym. Once he stopped, she tried to switch positions so that she could see the rest of the dance, but he held her firmly, one hand on each of her hips, facing him and the hall that led to the boys' locker room.

Something stirred in her chest like a miniature tornado kicking up dust. "What is it?" Gone was the uncomfortable tension from the first two hours they were there together. In its place, a different tension. Vivi wasn't sure how to label this one, so she laughed nervously. "Who is that teacher, anyway? He's so cringey."

"Vivi, I like you." He dropped his hands and tucked them into his back pockets. "There. I said it."

There was no reason for her to be shocked or surprised or unnerved. But she was. All of those feelings. And yet one other feeling crept up her spine and compelled her into him. It wasn't his dance moves. Not his quirkiness. Or smarts. Or the moroseness that took over him sometimes. Even months in, Vivi couldn't exactly pin down what it was about Eli. What made him hot. What made her so irrepressibly *into* him.

Vivi followed the compulsion, reached up, and grabbed the back of Eli's head and pulled it down to hers.

And she kissed him. Hard.

But she was in for an even bigger shock. Vivi had kissed several boys in her short years as a kissing girl, and it turned out that Eli was better than every single one.

~

AFTER THAT FIRST KISS, they kissed some more. Then they danced. Maybe she imagined it, but Eli's rhythm seemed to improve and they were glued to each other until the lights went on and the administrators and teachers shooed everyone home.

No one in their party had a full-blown driver's license yet. Only learner's permits. So, they huddled like nerdy underclassmen in a clump near the parking lot.

Nearly all of the other dancegoers had left in their own vehicles or with upperclassmen. Fewer underclassmen typically attended school dances, and those who did came and left singularly with their nervous parents.

Vivi's mom was also a nervous parent, of course. But she was as nervous about Vivi getting hurt or sick as she was about Vivi getting in trouble. This was a consequence of the Thing. The Thing was what had happened over two years prior, sending Vivi into the house of her father rather than her mother. But the Thing was a lone event. It, paired with the unreasonable conditions of living with Quinn, had worked together to force Vivi's hand. She understood all of this, but she still loved her mom. She was just figuring out how to respect her now.

Principal Ruthenberg came up behind their group. "You guys have a ride?"

Elijah relaxed his grip on Vivi's waist by a few degrees. "Yessir. Vivi's mom is coming to get us at ten."

The principal checked his watch. "I guess we wrapped things up a smidgen early. It's two minutes to ten."

"I shoulda just driven," one of the other boys

lamented, kicking a piece of gravel across the sidewalk. "I'm one week away from getting my license."

"There she is." Elijah pointed through the darkness. Sure enough, Quinn's black SUV rolled around the loop and toward where the group of six teenagers and Principal Ruthenberg stood, shivering in their too-light semi-formalwear.

"Hi guys!" Quinn hunched from her spot in the driver's seat, her blond hair bunched messily into a clip. Vivi knew her mom was *the hot mom*, and it was made even more painfully obvious when Quinn and the other mothers argued over who'd drive the kids to the dance, after talk of getting a limo had fizzled. Mr. Best had offered to drive Eli and Vivi, but Quinn protested that she'd like to drive them. The other two girls' moms had also wanted to drive, but the girls' *dates* wanted to ride in "Mrs. Fiorillo's." Vivi hadn't bothered to correct them, but Quinn had been quick to.

*You can call me Ms. Whittle. Or Quinn, I suppose.*

Vivi had never seen her mother as the type to try for *cool mom*, but there she was, telling fifteen-year-old boys to call her by her first name. Vivi all but gagged.

In the end, though, Quinn had driven everyone. Her SUV provided a third bench seat and, in all, there were seven passenger spots.

"How was it?!" Quinn asked as they started climbing in.

"Amazing!" Vivi's two friends sighed like Cinderella's stepsisters after brushing elbows with the prince.

Of course, Vivi agreed. But for her, that was true not because of *sick beats* or a cute DJ or the cool factor of bumping and grinding in the general facility of the varsity cheerleading team and football players.

For Vivi, the dance was amazing for an entirely different reason.

Eli squeezed her hand below her mom's eye level. Then they joined the other two couples in loading into the back.

~

THEY GOT HOME to a little late-night buffet, courtesy of Mrs. Best, naturally. Who else was as preoccupied with feeding children and decorating homes with pretty, sugary splendor like they were meant to attract victims? Now that Vivi thought about it, Mrs. Best very much reminded her of the old witch in "Hansel and Gretel." Even their new home, the one behind Vivi's, sort of resembled an overzealous gingerbread house. What with its licorice-red siding and crisscross-y gables. The brick edges and oversize wreath spraying across the front door.

Despite the pizza, tower of caramel apples, and a carafe full of hot cocoa nestled in a platter of bowls bubbling with marshmallows and cinnamon sticks, Elijah paled.

"Oh, geez," he muttered. "Is she still here?"

"Who?" Quinn asked. "Your mom?"

"Yeah. She always goes overboard."

But his complaint was lost on the ravenous and grateful group, Vivi included, as they dove into the spread.

"No, but she did all of this *and* came up with a great idea about sleeping arrangements."

The group groaned.

"Mom," Vivi argued, "we've already got a plan. We'll all sleep in the living room. Girls on the sofas and boys on the floor. No big deal." She pleaded her mother with intense eyes, knowing full well the effect her icy blues normally had on people.

But this time, it didn't work. Quinn's face remained unaffected and impassive as she replied. "Girls in the upstairs rooms. Boys down here. And that's that. I've made up the guest rooms. You can figure it out from there. If you need me, I'll just be in the kitchen. My editor agreed to come over and help me get some work done ahead of this week. Turns out he gets the whole teen chaperone thing."

Quinn turned on the heel of her Ugg slipper and strode into the adjoining room, where a man's voice greeted her.

One of the other boys, the one by the name of Landon, groaned. "I forgot my *dad* was coming."

Quinn was gone, so it was up to Vivi to hazard a guess. "Your dad is my mom's boss?" The pieces fell into place in her brain. Landon *Jericho*. Of course.

"Yeah. Forrest."

It made no sense. None of it. Not her mother's cool, calm, and collected tone. Not the perfect display minus Annette flitting about overprotectively. Not the hard-and-fast rule about girls upstairs and boys down.

And not Quinn's own late-night visitor.

Something akin to respect was growing in Vivi's heart. Respect, for the first time in a long time, for her very own mother.

Respect *and* maybe even awe.

# CHAPTER 16—QUINN

Learning that Forrest had a child had been nothing short of a shocker. Quinn had sworn he was single and childfree, even. But then, Saturday, after the moms and kids—and Roman—took a million photos, someone created a group chat to share those photos among the parents. And there he was on the list. Forrest Jericho.

She'd opened a second, private thread with him, asking why he happened to be in the photo-share.

Turned out, he had a son, Vivi's age, from a brief relationship fifteen years earlier.

Quinn asked why she hadn't known.

He'd sent a sheepish-face emoji and replied that Landon didn't want much to do with his dad these days. There'd been a falling out, of sorts, and Forrest was trying to respect the boundary.

It would be a questionable thing, except for the fact that Quinn had been there herself. She understood.

*Do you two ever see each other? Are you "no contact"?* she'd written.

Forrest said no. They were in touch. Just that Landon lived with his mom and preferred for her to do that parent stuff. Sometimes, the two guys would go fishing or hit the movies. But Forrest worried about being a fun-time dad and not a real father, so he toed the line, ensuring he didn't overstep Landon's mom's boundaries, either. It was a delicate thing, to be a dad on the outs but not out of the picture.

*The kids are having one big coed sleepover at my house after the dance*, Quinn wrote. *I'm overwhelmed. Do teenagers do this sort of thing here?*

He'd sent a laughing emoji and replied, *Do you need help? Someone to cover a shift, maybe?*

Quinn had smiled to herself and replied yes. Why hadn't she thought of that? But, would Landon mind?

Forrest had shot off a text to his son and got approval to show up and help. So, at about nine o'clock, he appeared at Quinn's front door with a bottle of wine and an additional two boxes of pizza. "For the kids," he said. "Figured with teenagers, you can never have too much."

"The wine, too?" Quinn took the bottle and smirked.

Forrest just laughed and followed her in.

They settled in the kitchen, and Quinn grabbed a pair of glasses, her hand trembling at the cupboard.

"I'd better rinse these." She took them to the sink and forced her breath to slow. Forrest did all of this to her. His reddish waves and freckles. The green eyes. He was nothing like Matt, her ex. And a little paunchy, even. Dad-bod paunchy, she now realized. Although, could you have a dad bod if you weren't a full-time dad? Quinn wasn't sure about that. But she *was* sure there was something undeniably attractive about Forrest.

"How's everything coming for Blue?" he asked, using the office abbreviation for Beverly's feature. In just the past couple of days, it had taken on a life of its own. Print news had long been struggling with its impending death, but Forrest had done everything in his power to stay ahead of online news trends and apps. He'd even had a developer create an app for the *Herald*. The website was up-to-date and impressive. The biggest issue still was monetization. No one wanted to pay for an online news subscription when they could just as easily grab gossip from their Facebook feeds.

Enter Quinn, whose job it was to drive tons of traffic to the *Herald*'s social media accounts. Beverly's feature could be a huge force in this, so both women had a lot on their plates to make it work. As for Forrest? Well, he'd been acting even more stressed out than usual. Fear seemed to be driving him. Fear that the feature would be a bust. Fear that it would take off, but he wouldn't be sure how to scale it or sustain it. Fear in general.

"It's coming," Quinn replied, joining him at her table with the glasses. He poured. "I plan to work on it tonight, as a matter of fact. It'll help keep me bright-eyed and bushy-tailed."

"You're worried the kids are going to hook up under your nose?"

"Who wouldn't be? They're teenagers."

"They're good kids. Even my rascal Landon and his buddy. Try-hards at times. But good kids."

Quinn silently wished she could say the same for Vivi. And just that silent wish washed her over in guilt. What a betrayal for her to think that of her own daughter. Vivi wasn't a bad kid. But if she wasn't a good kid— "Vivi is a good girl, too," she said. "But even good kids can make bad decisions. You know?"

"Even good adults can make bad decisions." Forrest lifted his glass. "To bad decisions," he toasted.

Quinn felt herself flush, the blood rushing up her neck in splotches and landing in her cheeks. What kind of a toast was *that*?

She withheld her glass in midair. "I don't think I can handle another bad decision from Vivi. Not after this summer." By now, Forrest already knew about the running away situation. What he may not have realized was just how much it had rocked Quinn's world. Even after the dust settled, the fear that Vivi would pull something like that again buzzed like chronic back pain in Quinn.

Forrest dipped his chin at her, and the boyish grin softened her nerves. "I wasn't talking about our kids."

IT TURNED out Forrest's idea of bad decisions was more similar to Quinn's than she'd have thought. Namely, getting work done under the influence of a generous glass of wine. They munched on a bowl of trail mix and each downed a glass of iced tea after the wine, then she cracked open her laptop before leaving him briefly to pick up the kids from the dance.

Their return home was less awkward than she'd pictured, maybe because she waved it off as help with work and with chaperoning. Teenagers were happy to see their parents as stiff geeks who'd rather while away the hours for their careers as opposed to nosey ones who overinvolved themselves in their children's lives. This was heartbreakingly evident in Elijah, who all but darted when he learned his mom had set up over half the buffet and decked the living room out with on-theme colors and ornamentation. Purple and black balloons, pumpkin and gourd tableaus—which was actually thanks to Quinn, who'd had them established in the entryway prior to the dance. Dishes of candy corn and roasted pumpkin seeds felt a little too Halloween-y—it wasn't meant to be a Halloween party, per se. But all of the kids loved it. Even Elijah let go of his irritation—or seemed to—by the time they settled in for their scary movie.

Come two in the morning, every last child was accounted for and really, truly asleep. The girls upstairs and the boys down.

By then, she and Forrest had finalized graphics for all social media posts, scheduled said posts, and prepared several ads to drive traffic to the upcoming feature *and* to the subscription page. The promise they agreed to offer was that while they'd get hints of the gossip in the social posts, they could only get the full story one of three ways:

One, subscribing to the print edition. There would be new write-ins each week, so if this week looked interesting, they could sub in the next.

Two, subscribing to the full-access version of the online edition.

And three, subscribing to Forrest's new (and maybe risky) My News app. This was a curated version of the *Harbor Herald*. It came at a monthly rate of $5.99 and would net subscribers up to three columns per week. They could opt in and out of features as they went, but the idea was that they were paying way less to get way less. If they subscribed to My News, they could elect to receive The House with the Blue Front Door column, and voila. The problem with this new idea was how much software development and coordination was involved, and Forrest would have to hire even more help if it took off. Once they hit more than fifty subs for this program, he'd do just that. If they never hit more than fifty, they'd eliminate it.

"I think we're ready." Quinn saved their roll-out plan to the cloud and closed her laptop. "You really don't have to stay all night. I'm out of beds."

"Hey now," he replied through a yawn, "I thought we were supposed to make some bad decisions tonight."

Quinn's gut clenched, her insides twisting and cramping almost instantly at his suggestion—or what she *thought* it was.

Panic must have been visible on her face because Forrest raised an eyebrow. "We just got a ton of work done. That's pretty much a good decision, right?"

"Well, it *is* past my bedtime," she reasoned, relaxing instantly when she realized his implication was only innocent. "At my age, that's a bad decision. Plus, there was the wine. I'm in for it."

"At your age?" A funny look crossed his face, like he had something more to say but thought better of it. This resulted in an awkward pause wherein Quinn wondered if she was supposed to tell him exactly how old she was.

Nervous and partly hoping to keep him there—in her kitchen, in her house—she did the thing that women north of forty weren't supposed to do. She revealed that she was, indeed, north of forty.

"Me, too. And it feels great, I might add."

"Feels great?" She gave him a look. "Isn't it all uphill from here?"

Forrest shook a finger at her. "That's how I know you're not a journalist or a writer."

Quinn frowned. "What?"

"Technically, if things are getting worse, they're going *downhill*, not uphill. This is the kind of BS I have to dwell on as an editor." He winced. "Sorry. I don't know—I don't know why I said that."

"Maybe to say out loud that you regret hiring me?" She meant it as a joke, but it fell short.

Forrest didn't notice. His gaze turned hard on her. "Why would I say that?" He shook his head. "Quinn, why would I *think* that?"

"I'm superfluous. There's a writer word for you." She tried for soft laughter, but it fell out like a sharp cackle. "Sorry. Ugh." Quinn pushed her fingers through her messy hair, tugging pieces loose around her face as if to cocoon herself within the embarrassment she'd caused.

"At first, I might have agreed. But Bev knows what she's doing. She knows what can make the business better, and she has a good eye for a good team member."

The phrase was a pinprick to her skin. *Team member.* Maybe Quinn flinched, because Forrest shifted his weight forward and touched the tip of her elbow with his hand. At this, she couldn't control herself.

Forrest whipped his hand back. "Sorry. I just—I just mean that I'm glad to work with you. Quinn, I really like working with you." He took a step back, and she wanted to grab him and pull him back closer at the same time that she just wanted him to leave. She hadn't been ready to spend hours—late-night hours—with her charming boss. But now that they had...

"I really like working with you, too, Forrest."

## CHAPTER 17—VIVI

Vivi woke up late the next morning, but not as late as the others. Before the other two girls got up, she stole into the bathroom to freshen up. It was critical that Vivi appear downstairs looking better than she actually did when she woke up, but not so good that anyone accused her of getting *dolled up*, as her Grams would say.

She brushed her teeth, naturally—even her tongue. Not that she and Eli would have a chance to sneak away, but she definitely didn't want him to think she had bad morning breath. After that, Vivi applied ample deodorant, double-checking that no pesky stubble had sprouted in the course of the last couple of hours. Satisfied that her clean shave from the after-noon before had held up, Vivi smudged on lip gloss and wiped smeared mascara from under her eyes. Lastly, she spritzed body spray around herself, sputtering out a cough in the plume of fragrance.

She then crept down the stairs, glancing at the grandfather clock on the wall by the door. Just past eight. Her eyes slid across the downstairs until she spotted a motionless form on the sofa. Unsure if it was Landon or Chase or Eli, she craned her neck over the furniture back when a voice from behind her gave her a start.

It was a man's voice.

Not a boy's.

The party guest on the sofa didn't stir, and Vivi wondered briefly if she should wake him or call up to her mom or investigate herself.

As she started back up the stairs, a second voice joined the man's.

Her mother's.

Her mother's *laughter*.

"Mom?" Vivi didn't bother to keep her voice down as she trotted back down the stairs and swung into the kitchen. Her eyes turned wide as she took in the view of who Vivi now knew to be both her mother's *boss* and Landon's *dad*. But Mr. Jericho's mere presence wasn't enough to confuse Vivi. It was the entire picture of the two of them. Quinn at the stove, flipping pancakes. Mr. Jericho standing very nearby, his elbow brushing against Vivi's mother's waist, even. He was moving bacon from a cookie sheet onto a paper-towel-sheathed platter.

Coffee bubbled into its pot in the far corner of the kitchen. Paper plates, napkins, cups and plastic utensils sat orderly across the table. One of the pumpkins and a few of the gourds had been moved to the table and flecked in maple leaves as if Mrs. Castle had been there, coordinating this breakfast just as she'd coordinated the late-night buffet.

Vivi was most amazed by the fact that her mother had yet to notice her presence. Quinn's overprotectiveness and suffocating parenting had been the prime cause for conflict in their relationship up to now. Her controlling behavior. Demands that Vivi shower and wash her hands and use hand sanitizer and not sit on her bed in her *street clothes*. All these things had propelled them apart.

But here was her mother, oblivious to Vivi. Not tearing up the stairs when she heard the name *Mom* waft across a light breeze. Not wringing her hands because Vivi had a fever. Not on her hands and knees scrubbing the throat of the toilet—that white bowel that nobody ever sees.

Quinn Whittle was lost in something that looked—to Vivi—a lot like happiness. Even more alarming? She wasn't lost alone or with Vivi. Or even with Mrs. Castle, who'd taken to Quinn like a girl takes to her new puppy dog.

"Mom?" Vivi tried again.

This time, Quinn and Mr. Jericho spun simultaneously, twisting in and somehow getting tangled in one another—him with the bacon tongs and her with the spatula. When Vivi caught her mother's eye, Quinn appeared to flush. But still, she laughed along with Mr. Jericho, who seemed equally sheepish.

"Hi, Viv." Stepping to the left and away from Mr. Jericho, Quinn revealed a tower of fresh pancakes waiting on a plate on the back burner. "Breakfast is hot. Want to wake up the others?"

"It's a little early for them, I think." Vivi made her way to the coffeepot and poured herself a steaming cup before sipping tentatively.

"Well, take a seat," Mr. Jericho suggested. "Early bird gets the worm, after all. You can have prime choice of bacon. We've got some burnt pieces and some rubbery ones. Not sure how that happened, to be honest."

Vivi suppressed a grin but she did sit down. "What is it with this place and newspapers?" she asked, involuntarily pulling the morning edition from the center of the table into the space in front of her. Her mother hadn't subscribed to the print version, but she did pay for the digital with her employee discount. Vivi didn't understand adults. Why pay for news when you could get it for free anywhere online? Or from social media?

"What do you mean?" Mr. Jericho asked. "Newspapers are sort of a thing everywhere if I'm not mistaken. I mean, don't get me wrong, it's been a couple of years since I've gotten out of Michigan, but from what I hear, people still like to read what's happening in their neck of the woods. Right?"

Vivi cringed at his awkwardness, but her mother recovered for him.

"When we moved in here, the former owner had left behind stacks and *stacks* of newspapers. I think Vivi is traumatized from having to drag them all to the roll-off."

"We didn't drag all of them," Vivi admitted. "Just most. We kept a few random piles in the garage in case we ever get bored again."

"Newspapers are partly informational and partly entertainment, after all," Mr. Jericho said. He was goofy but likable, she guessed.

Vivi couldn't help but reply with a little teenagerly mystique. "They can be other things, too."

"Oh yeah?" He set the heap of bacon down in the middle of the table, an expansive farmhouse thing recovered from the basement. *A Carlson piece* was how Quinn and Vivi came to refer to those salvaged items. His eyes narrowed on Vivi and he gave her a finger shake. "You'd make a great writer. You've got the element of suspense."

"I do want to be a writer," Vivi shot back, shaking out the newspaper expertly. "Maybe I'll write mysteries."

"You have to be careful, though, Viv," her mom admonished. "Good writers don't leave their audience hanging off of a cliff like you just did." She winked, and Vivi forwent a great opportunity at a massive eye roll.

"As if you didn't tell him about *that*," Vivi answered. "He probably knows."

"Knows *what*?" Mr. Jericho appeared genuinely dumbfounded.

"It's old news, quite literally," Quinn answered. "Vivi and Elijah came across an article among Carlson's old crap. It was written by Beverly back when she worked in Detroit. I guess she covered the disappearance of that local-ish woman, Temper? Miss Temper or something?"

"Temperance Temper."

Vivi whipped her head toward the newcomer's voice. Eli, of course. Looking adorably rumpled. It was highly unlikely he'd taken the extra time to do a little tidying up. More probably, he'd rolled out of bed and wandered in the direction of the voices. She wondered if he had morning breath and figured probably not. Eli was the sort to have packed his toothbrush or run home after everyone else had gone to bed. He'd probably flossed, brushed, and rinsed—in that order. Maybe he even kept a pack of those disposable toothbrushes in his pocket or something. Or maybe gum. He was always chewing gum.

Sure enough, when he joined her at the table, falling heavily into the chair next to Vivi, all she smelled was Eli, and that smell was dependably shampoo, mint—the gum—and the faint hint of cologne. Never having spied a bottle in his bedroom or bathroom, she suspected he didn't actually *wear* cologne. That he just naturally smelled fragrant. It was who he was. A clean, good-smelling, bad-dancing good kisser.

Vivi felt his hand tickle her knee beneath the table, and her heart leaped to her throat.

The adults, none the wiser—or indifferent—barreled ahead with all they knew about the Temperance case, which was precious little.

Quinn had peeled apart the paper. "There it is." She pointed for Mr. Jericho's benefit, and suddenly they had returned to a world of their own. In it, they gushed over the new big thing Quinn had been working on. Mrs. Castle's gossip stories, or whatever. It interested Vivi, but not as much as Eli right now.

Eli turned to her and dropped his voice. "I got a notification on my phone about Beverly Castle's story. Did you?"

She shook her head. "I don't subscribe."

"Well, read this." He showed her his phone, huddling his head close to hers. She regretted sipping on coffee after taking pains to brush her teeth, but Eli's screen seized her attention fully. She read it once. Twice.

Her eyes flashed to Eli's. "What did Beverly say back? How did she answer?"

He scrolled for her, and she read on.

*Dear Upset Parent,*

*I think most parents can relate to your problem here. I've been in your shoes in a similar way. Having a beef with your child's teacher—or rather, when your child has a beef with his teacher—it's a catch-22. Do nothing, and the problem persists. Do something, and the problem could worsen.*

*My advice to you is to first have your son take this up directly with the teacher if he hasn't yet. If he has, then it's your turn to email or call the teacher. You can explain the perception or explain the high stakes, but you should always remember to hold your child accountable first. That's what my mother always told me, and it's the same way I taught my daughter. Adults are more willing to work with young people who show personal responsibility. If all else fails, consider rounding up the troops. Surely if your son is right, then he won't be the only scorned male student, so to speak. But don't sit on this. From what I hear, college tuition doubles by the minute. In this modern world where we work hard to achieve equality, let us not forget that boys sometimes need extra help, too. Your son deserves the best. All of our sons and daughters do.*

"GEE-EEZ," Vivi jeered. "Harsh much?"

Eli squinted at her from behind his glasses. "Don't you see, Viv?"

"See what?"

"This article. You know who the mom is talking about."

"You mean the teacher?" She ventured another sip, this time keeping the cup in front of her mouth.

He retracted his phone, pocketed it, and raised his plate so it would meet with Quinn's spatula. "Thank you, Ms. Whittle." She added two pancakes to Vivi's plate, too, and to put her at ease, both kids helped themselves to a couple of pieces of bacon.

Vivi's mom smiled then returned to the kitchen island where Mr. Jericho had flattened out the big feature. They also had their phones on. From the sounds of it, Mr. Jericho had begun fielding texts with feedback. It sounded bubbly.

But Eli was anything but bubbly at the moment. "A teacher who favors the girls?" She thought hard, scrunching her face in an effort to catalogue the teachers she had and compare them against the teachers she'd only heard of. At last, Vivi shook her head. "I mean, *maybe* Mr. Belinger. But I only say that because you don't want to do the extra credit, so I figure you don't want to kiss up to him, and I *know* you, Elijah Best. You don't have patience for jerks."

Eli looked a bit taken aback at her tirade. A smile crawled up his left cheek, pushing his dimple into place and turning her insides to pancake batter. "You're wrong."

Vivi's face fell, but not for long. "Oh, you mean you *do* put up with jerks?"

He rolled his eyes and again she felt his hand on her knee, this time squeezing urgently. "It's not Belinger."

"The teacher?" Quinn had magically materialized back at the table, a cup of coffee dangling from one lithe hand. Her phone dangling from the other. "You know who it is?" Her eyes were wide and her mouth crooked. Not quite a smile. Not quite a frown. Behind her stood Mr. Jericho. His expression darker.

"It doesn't matter," he said. "This is that fine line we've talked about. You know, between gossip column and advice column. Bev's advice was spot-on. That's what counts."

Quinn turned to him. "What if this teacher is lowballing Landon, too?" She gestured to Eli. "Or Elijah? Shouldn't there be a bit of justice about this whole thing? I mean, they're *kids*, Forrest."

Mr. Jericho seemed to consider this point carefully, but Vivi replied. "Do you really want to know? Wouldn't that...change how he looks in your eyes?"

"Why would that matter? It's not like I know the guy. We hardly know anyone in town."

Eli chimed in. "Give it time, Ms. W."

"There's a phrase that comes to mind here," Mr. Jericho added thoughtfully. "Don't poop where you eat."

"You think I'm going to mount a witch hunt for this teacher? I'm not—" Quinn's face turned somber, serious. If Vivi knew one thing about her mom, it was that she was a rule follower. To "mount a witch hunt" was sure to send trouble back her way, and that would send Quinn over the top.

"Of course you're not. But even opening the can of worms, Mom. Is it *worth* it?"

Mr. Jericho cleared his throat. "Well, I actually meant that this teacher shouldn't be pooping where he eats, either."

All three turned their faces on him. "You're siding with me?" Quinn asked.

"Obviously," he answered. "You make a good point. Landon would never speak up if he had really earned an A but was handed a B. Or even a C. He probably wouldn't even notice, frankly. I've been a poor role model, I guess."

"He's not confrontational. It's not a bad thing." Quinn smiled at him then at Vivi and Eli.

"He doesn't pay attention. That's definitely a bad thing." Mr. Jericho let out a sigh.

Quinn took a breath. "Forget I asked who the teacher is. Maybe Bev's column is just what he or she needed as a reminder. Maybe things will change on Monday, even."

Mostly satisfied that they'd put the matter to rest, Vivi and Eli returned to their breakfast. Their hunger had suddenly kicked in. Quinn and Mr. Jericho returned to the kitchen island and the newspaper and their incoming texts of congratulations or of criticism, as the case could be.

But just as breakfast was feeling normal, the other four appeared in the doorway to the kitchen, mostly bleary-eyed and droopy. Not Landon, though. A fire lit up his eyes.

"Dad, did you *see* this?" He flashed his phone to his dad, whose face tightened. Vivi felt it all happen in slow motion, like when a toddler knocks over a glass of milk or a dog with muddy paws launches itself onto a cream-white sofa.

Mr. Jericho was about to respond. De-escalate, maybe. But it was too late.

Landon spilled the beans.

"I *knew* I got an A in that scumbag's class. This was my best quarter yet. I was *on fire*. I turned in everything! It was, like, weird. And, *boom*. Not an A but a C minus." Landon shook his head.

"Was it *your* mom who wrote in to the paper, then?" Vivi asked, now sucked in so hard that she could feel herself tremble with the gossip. It was a fun distraction from the heavier stuff that had been on her plate. You know, like the disappearance of Temperance Temper and the discovery of a skeleton in her boyfriend's backyard. Those kinds of heavy things.

"Of course not. My mom would write in and tell the turd to give me a D if she had the chance." He sneered and shook his head then sank into the spot next to Eli. "And you of all people probably know what a loser this guy is, too."

"Me?" Eli squeaked.

"Yeah. Your mom and dad basically *gave* him that house, right? I mean he obviously got it for a steal. What a cheap-o. Now I'm *definitely* contesting my quarter one grade. No doubt about it." Landon just shook his head amusedly as he stabbed pancake after pancake and flopped them onto his plate, pouring syrup like he was soaking his front lawn and clicking his tongue like a middle-aged mom.

"So, this teacher," Quinn interceded while the last three kids took their seats and groggily fumbled to serve themselves, "the one who plays favorites, is a...a *client* of Annette and Roman Best?"

Landon answered through a mouthful, his amusement welling up again as he jerked his thumb toward Eli like Eli was in on some joke. "A *client*," Landon guffawed through the chewed-up bacon-and-pancake-and-syrup mixture. Then he swallowed and turned his attention from Quinn to Vivi and back again. "He's your new *neighbor*."

# CHAPTER 18—ANNETTE

Annette and Roman awoke on Sunday to a quiet house. Typically, Elijah was a quiet boy, but his parents could feel his absence this morning. As though he were a ghost, Annette *sensed* him, but then again, maybe that's because he was in the house just behind her own. What should be a comforting thought actually set her on edge.

It wasn't that Quinn was an unfit chaperone. It wasn't that Annette distrusted her son, either. Was it Vivi? The sweet-but-spicy teen girl who had Elijah twisted around her little finger?

Or was there something else, bubbling beneath the surface of her skin? This, probably, was anxiety calling. Anxiety had visited Annette in brief waves in her life, never taking root like an infestation. Nothing like Quinn. And no depression, either. That was for

Beverly. Not even a moroseness could taint one of Annette's days, unlike Jude, who very obviously battled against that very urge.

Annette didn't like the bad feeling thrumming low in her body. It made it hard to get out of bed; it made her feel silly and spoiled. It made the day drearier. Or was that her new house? With its minimal natural light and western exposure? The best thing to do was to sit on her back porch, facing the sunrise.

That's just what she needed. A little vitamin D.

"Ro?" she called, tying off her house robe and padding into the kitchen.

Roman was walking in from the front door, newspaper in hand. Hazelnut coffee wafted heavily in the air. Her favorite. In the toaster glowed two pieces of cinnamon-raisin bread. Roman hated cinnamon-raisin bread. They didn't even keep it in the house because Annette would tear into it and live with regret for a week.

"Morning." Roman adjusted his glasses and smiled warmly. "It's just us, you know."

"I know," Annette replied warily.

He tapped the rolled newspaper against his palm. "How'd you sleep?"

"Surprisingly well."

"Yeah." He gave it a moment's thought. "I can't sleep when he's gone, either, usually. But I think we're exhausted."

She nodded then poked her finger toward the toaster. "My bread?"

Roman gave an impish look. "I think you earned it."

"And hazelnut coffee? When did you go to the store? I thought we were doing only bare necessities for a while?"

"I had a little good news," Roman revealed.

At this, she perked up. "Good news?" In the Best household right now, good news could mean only one thing.

"I talked to my mom this morning."

"Your mom?" Annette had tried to accept that she'd be entertaining her in-laws this week. She'd even prepared to give them some things to do that could turn them helpful, after all. This was more out of self-preservation than as a favor to Roman, but...she planned to try.

"They're postponing their trip here. They agreed that it's bad timing and if there's anything they can do to help, they can do it from afar as easily as they can do it from Bertie's."

Annette frowned. "Roman, I *want* your parents to visit, you know." She found herself to be sincere in this admission, and it felt a bit odd.

He gave her a sideways look. "You're only saying that because I bought your favorite coffee and bread."

"And even brewed it and popped it in the toaster,"

she added playfully as she pulled the toast out and worked apple butter into it. No better way to start the day. "But seriously. I always enjoy their company. I'm just—I mean, *we're all* just a little overwhelmed, I think."

"That's why I invited them to begin with, you know. To help?"

She knew. She did. "What if we make special Thanksgiving plans? Would your mom go for that? I know she likes to host your brother's and sister's families, but—"

"She'd love that," Roman cut her off and wrapped her in a hug from behind. Warmth—warmth of body and soul—melted Annette.

She finished preparing her toast and took a generous bite before swiveling in her husband's arms to face him. "Okay, what's going on here?" she accused, her eyes slits and her lips sticky from the butter.

He planted a kiss on her forehead and released her. "Let's talk on the back porch. The sun is coming up, and I don't want to miss it."

~

ROMAN SET about making himself grits and then a fresh pot of regular coffee while Annette carried her breakfast and the paper to the back porch.

Once there, Annette felt peace run through her

veins. The morning's anxiety was like a nightmare from which she'd woken, and now she could enjoy a little *me time.*

She turned to her favorite section of the paper to recall that Beverly Castle's new feature was running in today's edition. Lifestyle was Annette's go-to in the paper, but now the Sunday lifestyle section would be particularly fun. The first two write-ins felt like the usual small-town problems. The Christmas gala—Annette did miss that. It was an excellent networking event. She and Roman had even participated generously in the home tour. Then the teacher complaint. Annette typically gave little credence to parents who complained about teachers. But she knew this indifference came from the fact that Annette had never once had to intervene on Elijah's behalf.

Still, she was entirely curious about *who* this biased teacher might be. The infamous Belinger? Who allowed his students to report on the macabre? Highly unlikely. Elijah liked him just fine.

Could it be Jude? She *did* have a beef with men. Look at how she acted toward a kind, interested man like Dean Jericho, after all.

Annette's interest in the school pseudo-scandal dissolved when her eyes landed on the third and final write-in. Her eyes flew through the question, skipping over some to get to Beverly's reply. Gut clenching and twisting, Annette forced herself to read it.

. . .

Dear Neighbor,

*Do you love your partner? That's the first thing I'd wonder. If the answer is yes, then I suppose the next thing to find out is a tad bit trickier. Does your partner still love you? If yes to both, proceed with caution. If you've fallen out of love, then this decision should be an easy one. If your partner has, I'm sorry. It will be a rough road, but what you can and should do is keep reaching out to others for support. In times of need, there's little sense in bottling away your hardship. Trust me when I say heartache keeps better than Grandma's preserves. Good luck.*

Tears welled up in Annette's eyes. She couldn't recall the last time she'd *cried*, for heaven's sake. She brushed them away and set the paper down on her lap.

"Annie?" Roman appeared at her side with his own coffee in hand. "Is everything okay?"

Annette swallowed past the growing lump in her throat. "Roman," she answered, keeping her gaze on the hazy sunrise. "Do you love me?"

# CHAPTER 19—BEVERLY

Sunday morning, Beverly woke up well rested for the first time in a long time. She'd forgotten to take her evening pills, instead falling asleep easily—and even in her bed. And not too late, either.

After enjoying an impromptu lunch with Darry, the two had done their shopping quasi-together. It would have been an uncomfortable thing if Beverly weren't so dang comfortable with him. And him with her, she supposed. They'd parted ways in the parking lot of the market, settling together on a breakfast time at Beverly's house.

The next morning, Darry would be Beverly's very first planned visitor since the wake. This should have caused her panic. It should have sent her canceling and downing a bottle of wine and half a bottle of her pills. But she did none of that.

Instead, she'd arrived home and gone directly to Kayla's bedroom.

Another first.

There, she'd fallen onto the bed like Kayla used to do, a giddy girl with a cozy four-poster that they found at the Penny House one lucky summer. Over winter break one particular snowy year, they painted her walls peach. Kayla had immediately regretted it, and Beverly, too. They'd repainted the whole of it all over again, the second time yellow. It complemented everything else in Kayla's room. The cornflower-blue comforter and matching curtains—made expressly by Gramma Bertie. The blue rag rug and the blue afghan. Also Gramma Bertie.

Beverly realized for perhaps the first time that a lot of who Kayla was had come from Beverly's own mother. And yet, despite that fact and so many others...Bertie had handled it all so well. It had made Beverly angry with her for a while. How her mother could go on. Then that anger had turned inward, like a pistol pointing itself at one's own heart. How could *Beverly* have gone on? How *had* she?

She had, hadn't she? She'd lived her life, there in that very house. She hadn't killed herself like she'd always expected in such a situation. It was a thought that crossed her mind daily, of course. It was a thought that had crossed her mind long before Kayla died. Beverly could remember those early, innocent days when she wondered privately, *What would I do if Kayla died?* The answer had come quickly. *I'll die, too.*

But Beverly was still alive now. Eleven months later, she was alive and breathing heavily on her back in her dead daughter's unmade bed. As unmade as it had been on that tragic day the year before.

Bertie had come in there before the wake, but Beverly had caught her in the act. *I want to make it look nice!* her mother had cried.

*It DOES look nice!* Beverly had sobbed. *What are you TALKING ABOUT! Dammit, Mom, it's PERFECT!*

*Don't you use the Lord's name in vain, Beverly Ann. Think about Kayla. Think of her soul. Think of* your *soul, Bev.* They'd collapsed on the floor together, but Beverly's sobs had drowned out anything more her mother'd had to say. She could have slapped her, probably.

Now, though, Beverly didn't cry, no. Instead, she looked around, dry-eyed and breathing heavily. *Alive.*

"I had lunch with Mr. Ruthenberg today, Kay," she whispered into the corners of the room, searching them for a response. A ghost. A sign. Nothing came. She went on. "I would have divorced your dad. Maybe I should have. His stuff is gone—you probably know. I bet you can see everything. The dogs are good."

Stream of consciousness. Word vomit. It kept coming, and it felt *good*. "I have a new feature for the paper. It's interesting. People write in with problems or questions or even gossip, and I just give them my thoughts. Easy, huh? It's harder than you'd think, actually. Kay, I feel the eyes of the world on me now. I feel *your* eyes on me."

A shuddering breath racked Beverly's body, but she resisted its pull. "What do you think about Mr. Ruthenberg? I know you didn't have much to say about him. That's good, right? Only the troublemakers have much to say about their principal. Kayla, I don't know what to do with my feelings about Darry—I'll just use his first name. I'm jumbled up inside. I…I need a sign, I guess. I need permission, Kay."

The sob rolled like a ball from the base of her stomach up to her chest and hung in her throat. A wrecking ball. She bore down on it. "Have you seen the new girl on our street? Vivi. I don't know what you'd have thought of Vivi. She's loud. Not her voice. But as a person. I know you never liked Eli *like that*, but it seems like those two might date. I'm sorry. Should I be sorry, Kay? Are you happy for him? I think you are. I know I am, even though it's not my business."

Beverly sucked in a big gulp of air, and that wrecking ball lost its traction, sliding back into her chest.

She pushed up into a sitting position. "Kayla. I'm going to make your bed today. And maybe tomorrow, I'll dust. Or vacuum. And after that, do you know what I'm going to do, Kay? I'm going to pick fifteen of your things to keep. Just fifteen. One for every year of *you*.

This won't count pictures, sweetheart. But once I have those fifteen, then I'm going to do something I have to do if I'm going to live.

"My sweet Kay, I can't stay in this blue house. You don't live here anymore, and I can't, either. I wanted you to be the first to know. Because after today, I'm signing on with Eli's mom and dad. I haven't told them yet, but I have to find a different place to live, Kay. I hope you understand, sweet girl. Oh *God*." The sob clogged her throat again, sinking its fangs into the back of her tongue and tugging it until she gagged and flew to the window, pushing it open and gulping at the cold October air.

The chill stung her lungs, but she was too far gone and had no choice but to let the heaving, howling moans consume her.

Still crying, Beverly crawled underneath her daughter's covers and wept there until she fell asleep.

~

BEVERLY AWOKE WELL RESTED at four o'clock, and—another first—she awoke *aware* that Kayla was dead. She awoke without that brief, elated moment where everything felt like a nightmare. The dogs had found their way into the room and had guarded Beverly during her deep nap. Now they stirred and seemed confused to be in Kayla's bedroom. But she was not confused. She was calm. Surefooted.

Her eyes raw red and her stomach sore from the racking wails, Beverly did what she'd set out to do. She made Kayla's bed.

Then she clapped for Sandy and Danny, and the three of them left the room—door closed—and toured the rest of her house together. It was a mess, truthfully. And she knew she wasn't going to pull it together in time for the next morning.

Still, if her admission to Kayla—about moving—was the plan, then she might as well get a bit of a start now. With the first feature set to print, she didn't have anything else to do.

But first, she had an idea.

She picked up her phone.

Darry answered on the first ring. "Everything okay?"

"Yeah," she replied. "I just—is there any way we can make a slight change to tomorrow's plans?"

He let a brief pause take its breath before answering. "Bev, we don't have to do breakfast tomorrow if you're not comfortable with it. The last thing I want is to make you uncomfortable. I'm sorry if I have already, I—"

"No, no. I *definitely* want to meet," she insisted, clear-headed now even with the beginnings of a headache coming on. "Anyway, I just know that my neighbors will be pounding away at my door tomorrow morning once they get their papers." She laughed nervously. This was something of a fib. Beverly didn't think any of her neighbors would trespass on her privacy like that. She was sure of one thing: Jude, Annette, and Quinn had all been entirely respectful of the space Beverly had needed. In fact, they were part of the reason Beverly was feeling wishy-washy about moving. The main reason, of course, was that she'd be leaving Kayla's home. But her fifteen-belongs plan was supposed to account for that, as well as Beverly's conviction that Kayla's home wasn't in the house with the blue front door.

It was in Beverly's heart. And there, it would stay.

But interestingly, Beverly knew the other thing that pulled her back from putting the house on the market *right now* were those budding friendships. Did she really want to leave the street just as the girls were growing close with one another?

"Want to come to my place?" Darry asked. She would, but then that would scream *romantic breakfast*, and Beverly did not want a romantic breakfast. She wanted breakfast with an old friend whom she happened to still have the seeds of a crush on.

"Actually, would it be totally crazy to meet somewhere else?"

"Like at a diner?" He sounded as nervous about

that proposition as she was, but no. That wasn't her idea, either.

"How about something private, but not too private," she suggested.

"What do you have in mind?"

Beverly grinned. She could just imagine what her mother was going to think. "How about Bertie's B&B?"

~

AFTER CLEANING for two hours while listening to the Hallmark Christmas radio station, Beverly decided to take the dogs for a walk. Another—you guessed it —*first*.

When she got home, she took a long, hot shower, made a cup of chamomile tea, watched *You've Got Mail*, and then put herself to bed with a book she'd been meaning to read for at least two years. It was Tina Fey's memoir, and Beverly even let herself laugh out loud a time or two. Eventually, the dogs made their way up into bed with her, her eyes got heavy, and she fell asleep with the book dangling from her hand.

It was the best day Beverly had had in a while. But what she didn't know was that the next day would be even better.

~

"HE'S COMING *HERE*?" Bertie Gillespie wailed. "*Now?*"

"Mom, relax. It's not a meet-the-parents thing. You *know* Darry. And it's not a holiday brunch. It's French toast on a Sunday. And *I'm* the one cooking. You just go turn the beds or whatever you have to do. Don't mind us."

"Well, if you don't need me, then why are you having him *here*? And why didn't you call me first?" Her mother was flailing her hands about herself, then tying and retying her apron—a ratty old thing she wore out of sheer habit. It added to the B&B charm, she'd say anytime Beverly suggested she upgrade.

"I didn't want you to do anything. I *know* you, Mom."

Bertie finally propped each hand on a hip. "What's the meaning of this whole thing, anyway? Is it a *date*, Bev?" She whispered the last question and raised a black eyebrow suspiciously. But her mouth was the giveaway. A trembling smile fighting against itself. Bertie knew better than to ask Beverly a question like that.

"It's *not* a date. It's breakfast. With a friend. Period."

~

DARRY ARRIVED EXACTLY ON TIME.

"I got the paper. I mean, I'm sure you probably have

like a hundred copies. But I figured I'd frame my own. Who knows? You could be the next Barbara Walters."

She served their food and poured him a coffee then settled into the seat adjacent at the dining table. The B&B guests had already left for the morning, doing whatever Harbor Hills tourists did. "It's not that kind of thing. Barbara is a journalist. She does the tough stuff."

"I'd argue that what you're doing is way tougher. I mean, who wants to play mediator to a whole town of people who know each other and have beef with one another? You *know* these people, too. You've got the hard job, I think."

Beverly's chest swelled at that. She agreed with him, but the challenge was the thing making this assignment perfect for her. It gave her something to chew on and work at and distract her while keeping her close to reality, too.

"We've already got emails coming in about every single one of the questions. Lots of new questions, too. Some follow-ups, even." She glowed over this.

"Oh, yeah?"

Beverly pulled out her phone. "Lots of people want to bring back the Christmas thing. Some even have good ideas. The affair was a hot topic. Very heated. People either think the cheater should die or get a second chance. No real in between there, surprisingly."

"Is that so surprising?" Darry kept his gaze on his food.

She paused with her coffee in midair. "What do you mean?"

Darry shook his head, swallowing a bite. "I just mean...love is more complicated. It's never that black and white."

Silence took place in their conversation while both stared away, sipping their coffees and pretending that Darry was talking about people they didn't know.

"The responses to the school question have been interesting." She meant the comment as a bridge to a new topic. Beverly didn't necessarily desire to talk about high school politics. But Darry's head snapped to attention.

"What do you mean? How so?"

"Oh, just that, well, it seems that one question happened to represent a slew of parents—or their children, I suppose." She didn't want to get back into it. She'd already given Darry a piece of her mind about confronting teachers who'd earned themselves valid complaints. But then, wasn't that the question to begin with? Whether this particular complaint was valid?

Darry's face hardened. "Really? You mean other parents wrote emails to you about the exact same situation?"

"Do you think it's more than one teacher?"

"No." He shook his head. "I hope not, it's just—"

"Darry..." Her voice was low. "Maybe you should

pursue it. If you know who the parent is, then I take it you know who the teacher is?"

He pushed his hands through his hair until it stood on end. "Bev, it's just—" A sigh puffed up his face and he glanced around the otherwise empty dining room.

"Don't worry"—she smirked—"anyone else who happens to be here isn't a local."

Softening mildly, he continued. "We've been down this road before. A false accusation was made against a teacher. He lost his job. Threatened to sue the district and the family. And I don't blame him. Being a teacher is hard enough, Bev. Plus, do you know how often parents get up in arms about stuff like this? *Every single day*. The fact that this particular mother took it to your column is less suggestive of the authenticity of her *claim* as it is—" He stopped midsentence.

Beverly cocked her head. "Say it. Go on. The fact that this mother took her story to the paper just shows how much of a gossip rag the *Herald* is."

Darry returned an impassive stare. "I wouldn't put it that way, but you *are* inviting this, Bev. For better or worse, you're stirring the pot."

Ice sluiced through her veins, stilling her heartbeat for a moment too long. When she opened her mouth to reply, nothing came out. It was dry and cold.

He doubled down. "You've got the right idea. People need to vent. But at whose expense? That's all I'm saying. Your responses to these people are perfect, but...like I said, Bev. I've been down this road before, and it nearly ruined a teacher's life. He changed *careers* over it."

Beverly found her voice, shaky though it was. "What? And what *happened*? How come I don't know about it if it 'ruined his life'?" She clawed air quotes at Darry, her anger bubbling over. How could Beverly have been *attracted* to Darry? How could she have thought there might be a glimmer of something there, distant though it may have been?

How did he *not* know that he was supposed to use kid gloves with her? Everyone else did. Everyone else... The rest of the thought swallowed Beverly down.

Everyone else let her do whatever the hell she wanted ever since the accident. Consequence free, Beverly flopped around like a fish.

Or had they? Had that only been what Beverly *wanted* other people to do? Treat her like she might break?

Well, she might. And right now, she *would*. Tears pricked the corners of her eyes and she let them spill down her cheeks, coursing like miniature streams through the makeup she'd had enough energy to apply that morning. She never should have worn makeup. She never should have met Darry for breakfast. She never should have started this new feature.

It would all end. She'd call Forrest and tell him it was off. Maybe she'd quit. Maybe she'd give up.

But...

A thought commandeered her miserable mind. Grief could drown her.

It could change her.

It could ruin her.

But it wouldn't kill her.

Not yet, at least.

"There's a story there," she shot back, ferocity returning to her voice and fire to her eyes. Darry would have to fight back. But he wouldn't win.

"You were in Detroit back then. It was years ago, Bev. You didn't hear about it, because he managed to grab the story himself and shake it till it died. He took control of the narrative, Bev. And you know what? I don't blame him. After what they said, I'd have done the same thing. If I didn't kill myself first."

She glowered at him. "What happened?"

"That's not my story to tell, Bev. Like I said—what happened was horrible. He managed to change the story—to bury the lie and live the truth, and it's not my story to tell."

Beverly knitted her eyebrows together and thought of all the men she knew. Who, living among the innocents of Harbor Hills, had had this secret? And *how* had she missed it? Even living in Detroit? "Darry," she pleaded, "will you tell me who it is? I mean, you want me to believe the best about your teachers, right? Give me a chance to see for myself."

"You can't just take my word for it, can you?" He shook his head. "Stubborn as a mule. You always were. You wanted to live life on your terms. But you can't do that forever, Bev." Even though what he said was harsh, his eyes were forgiving. His lips upturned in a playful grin.

"I know that better than anyone," she replied, and she meant it. And he knew that she meant it. "If you feel so strongly that my column is exploitative and melodramatic, that it's a gossip piece and little more, then you'll stand by the fact that this teacher isn't playing favorites, right?"

"I didn't say that..." He held up his hands beggingly. "I said communities are quick to condemn teachers and accept rumors. That's what I said. It happened before, and I don't want it to happen again."

"Who is the teacher this time?" she asked, pressing her hands down on the table.

"I'm not sharing that, Bev."

"Okay, then fine. Who was the teacher last time?" But even as she asked it, the answer came to her on an addled cloud. She'd known all along. She'd known *him* all along. Everything made sense. Everything came together.

"Never mind," she whispered. "I already know."

# CHAPTER 20—QUINN

Tad Beckett played favorites.

Who didn't?

The world was full of favorites. Teachers weren't immune to that pull of humanity. Tad seemed nice enough. Looked younger, maybe. That could factor in. But after the kids finished breakfast and started on their journeys home, Forrest lingered behind with his son in the living room. They were engaging in a heated conversation when Quinn dared to join them.

"Everything okay?"

Forrest glanced up, his face streaked in something akin to discomfort. "We have to go. Landon's got homework for tomorrow, and I promised his mom I'd drop him home by noon."

"Oh." Quinn felt inexplicable disappointment creep in.

"See you tomorrow, Quinn."

~

AFTER THAT, everyone was gone and it was just Vivi and Quinn.

They sat, both listless, at the dining table. "You can take a nap if you want, sweetheart." She reached across to tuck a strand of Vivi's hair behind one ear.

Vivi thwarted the gesture with a flinch.

Quinn reeled. "Sorry."

"Mom, are you *seeing* him?"

"What?"

"Seeing Mr. Jericho? *Dating* him?"

"No," Quinn spat back. "Why would you even say that?" A stupid remark if ever there was one. Why *wouldn't* Vivi—a sharp, insightful, blossoming young woman—notice if another woman was interested in a man? Of course she would.

"Landon says his dad talks about you sometimes."

"What?" Quinn made a face. "Landon doesn't even *live* with his dad. *I* didn't even know Forrest had a son until yesterday!" As if that would explain anything.

"He said so last night." Vivi looked thoughtful. "Do you know why his dad doesn't have custody?"

"They had a falling out. It just...it's just how they've got things set up. Like you and me and Matt."

Vivi rolled her eyes. "Yeah. Whatever."

"What's with the sudden attitude, Viv? Are you tired? Did you eat enough for breakfast?" Even to Quinn, a nap sounded good right then.

But Vivi pushed out of her chair and hovered only a moment near her mother. "How do you *not* see, Mom?"

"See what?" Quinn's stomach lurched.

"Even Eli's noticed, and he doesn't care a fraction of the amount that I care."

"What are you talking about, Viv? Notice what?"

"She never told you, did she?" Vivi's eyes widened. Sudden realization washed her face out to the color of her hair.

"Who never told me *what*?" Quinn stood and gripped the edge of the table, bracing herself against a wave of anxiety. A tidal wave of it.

Vivi simply shook her head. "Never mind. I—I need to work on my extra credit assignment. I'm going over to Eli's."

"Temperance? You're still on that?"

"Yeah. We have a *huge* lead."

For whatever reason, Quinn had the urge to ask an unrelated question. "Viv, wait."

"What?"

"Mr. Beckett. Does he—does he play favorites like they said?"

Vivi shrugged. "Probably. I don't know because I'm not a teacher's pet."

Quinn's insides settled, but she had one more lingering question now that she'd gotten the hard one out of the way. "What's your big lead on the Temperance Temper thing?"

Rounding her mouth into a tight knot, Vivi seemed to consider how to answer. "I found something."

"What did you find?"

"A letter."

"Where? Who wrote it?"

"A woman whose name starts with T."

"Temperance?"

"Maybe," Vivi replied furtively.

Quinn blinked. "Show it to me."

## CHAPTER 21—VIVI

Reluctantly—though why she was reluctant, she couldn't say—Vivi pulled a tattered envelope from her backpack in the front hall. She didn't pass it to her mother. Instead, clutching it against her chest, she spoke slowly. Carefully.

"I found it by accident, actually. Remember those filing cabinets you had me go through?"

"I thought you were going to trash everything."

"Well, I didn't." Vivi kept the envelope pressed to her chest like it was worth hundreds of dollars. Maybe it was. "I thought where I found this one, I'd find more. But I didn't. Just this one." She shook her head. "There's no send date or even year. And the names are really vague. But there are two."

"Two names?"

Vivi nodded, ran her tongue over her lips, and slid

the fragile, yellowed page from its fragile, yellowed shroud. Centered at the top of the paper was a shadowy, embossed letter *T*.

Her mother didn't hold out a hand to take it from Vivi, so she simply read aloud.

"'My dear B., I received the one-way bus ticket to H.H. under the assumed name as is our plan. *Thank you*. I will keep my promise, even though I disagree with you. No one will know. I understand your reasons, I do. But just because one *understands* something doesn't mean one *believes* in it. Nonetheless. I believe in you. I believe in *us*. I'll see you November 1. Just confirming the address: 696 Apple Hill Lane. No need to reply unless I've got something wrong. I hope I don't. I fear, however, that it's *all* wrong.'"

Vivi looked up at her mother before letting her eyes fall back to the bottom of the unlined stationery. "'Your true love, Tippy.'"

# CHAPTER 22—ANNETTE

It was past noon on Sunday, and Annette had a fresh perspective for the week ahead. Changes were in store for the Best family. Big changes.

Roman had left to get some paperwork going. Annette was considering the fact that she really *would* be stuck in this red cottage, probably. And that was okay. It would all be okay. It had taken her the morning to feel convinced, but now she was.

Her current next move was to do a little writing of her own, spurred on, naturally, by this bright, shining new feature of darling Beverly.

Annette set her laptop up on the kitchen counter, fixed herself a midday coffee, pulled on her coziest, most comforting sweater, and opened a blank document.

In it, she detailed her situation, taking care to

include the involvement of a whole other family. The implications concerning her son, Elijah, and how the whole thing would affect her future. Roman's future. Hell, the future of Crabtree Court and Harbor Hills and—she was getting carried away. But these *were* the sorts of things that could erupt a small town like a volcano. *These* were the things to send magma oozing over perfectly adjusted American families. Some might even say that was the worst part—the oozing magma. That initial burst was a shock, sure. But it didn't touch that many. Not like that pesky magma. The aftershocks of one single family's personal scandal.

She reread her words, combing back through her version of events to ensure accuracy. Satisfied that her account would hold up in a court of law—how dramatic—Annette then opened her email, cross-referenced the address she'd found in the newspaper ad, provided a brief introduction of herself and her circumstances, then attached the document she'd written.

Finally, she sent the whole shebang, and just as she got that little alert indicating that the email had been successfully sent, the doorbell rang.

~

QUINN AND VIVI stood on the Bests' front porch.

"Hi, you two." Annette managed a wide smile but then it occurred to her that Quinn never showed up alongside Vivi. Maybe without her, sure. Or maybe sometime after her, to call her daughter home for supper. But never together. Annette's smile faltered, and she looked her friend up and down. "Oh, my Lord." Her hand flew to her mouth. "Is it that teacher?"

Quinn and Vivi exchanged an unreadable look.

"Do you *know* him, sweetheart? Is there more to the story?" Annette's eyes widened at the promise of a little *juice*. She'd felt fairly underwhelmed with the *ye olde teacher plays favorites* gripe. What human being on earth didn't have favorite people? Teachers were human, too.

Vivi replied, "Actually, I wanted to show Eli something for our project."

Annette's face fell. "Oh. Sure. You know where to find him." Vivi squeezed past her, but Quinn remained on the front porch, her eyes blinking a mile a minute and her fingers working together like she was playing piano in midair. "Quinn," Annette whispered. "What's wrong, hon?"

"It's just—I mean, I *do* think there's more to this teacher story, and for whatever reason Vivi is *so* wrapped up in the Temperance Temper thing, and I'm beginning to wonder if it's connected with whatever is happening with that teacher. You know, from Beverly's column." She paused only for a quick breath and to tuck a strand of her hair behind her ear before her blinking and tapping and talking resumed. "Landon Jericho was at my house last night. He pointed a finger at someone—I mean at a specific teacher. I got a bad feeling about it. And then Forrest—he was so gung-ho on covering some make-believe scandal at the school. That was when I started working there. He and Beverly had words about it. I remember it because it made me feel a little nervous about Vivi going there. I just...I have a bad feeling about something. Like...ever since you moved, it's like there isn't a new family next door. It's like there's a *ghost* next door. It's...weird, Annette. I *sound* weird, and I know I'm tired, and I know I'm just a worrywart but—"

Annette glanced back into the house then closed the door. "Small spaces, big echoes," she said in a hushed voice then indicated two white rocking chairs squished into one corner of the squat porch. "Sit. *Sit*."

They both waited a beat, and then Annette went ahead and asked. "First of all, who's the teacher? Don't tell me it's Jude."

"Landon seems to think it's..." Quinn's face pinched. "*Tad Beckett*."

Now it was Annette's turn to blink. She must have misheard. "Tad Beckett. As in...the man who lives in my house?"

Quinn nodded. "And that's not all. Vivi found this letter in Carl Carlson's old stuff. It's from a woman named Tippy, and it's extremely eerie. Vivi said there was another thing she'd found, too, but she couldn't tell me." Pain streaked the woman's face and her tics were set ablaze.

"A letter?" Annette's head was swelling with too much information...and not enough. Had Vivi spilled the beans on the body? "Let's start from the beginning. You heard from Landon Jericho that Tad Beckett is the teacher that woman was complaining about? That Tad plays favorites with his female students."

Quinn gave another nod.

"Okay, and that's uncomfortable because...Vivi has him? For a class?"

"Yes, she does. But it's not just the favorites thing. It's more than that."

"What do you mean? Just that he lives next to you, and now you feel it's a little too close for comfort? Remember, Quinn, before he lived next door, he lived behind you. That was probably worse."

Quinn returned a look.

"Okay, so you've got a bad feeling with him being next door. Fine. Like a ghost." Annette licked her lips. "Plus, the Tippy thing."

"The Tippy thing." Quinn didn't say this as confirmation of what Annette said. But as something else. Like she was trying out the words for herself. *The Tippy thing*.

Annette pursed her lips. "You know what, Quinn?"

She stood from the chair. "I have a lot to do this afternoon. Some paperwork to prepare. Roman and I had a long talk this morning—we're...well...I hate to ask you this, but can you and I get together another day?"

Quinn's eyes went wild again, blinking so quickly that it looked painful. She was bordering on a nervous breakdown. Annette grabbed her hand. "Listen, Quinn. The Tippy thing—leave Vivi and Eli to work on that. As for Tad, he's harmless, I'm sure. I'll shoot Darry a message, though. I mean, it can't hurt if there are extra eyes on the guy." Annette thought of something. "And you know what? I'm going to call Forrest. He'll stay with you. Until you feel better. He can sleep in your downstairs guest room. I won't take no from you or from him." Annette made a shooing gesture. "I'll call you when I get through this paperwork. We'll have something to celebrate then, hon. I promise!"

Confused-looking and frowning, Quinn wandered off the porch and down the side yard back toward her own house.

And Annette tore through the house directly into Elijah's bedroom. "You're right," she snapped to Elijah. "I don't think the Becketts called the police."

"Why not?" Vivi asked, immediately in the loop, even though her poor, addled mother was hanging precariously outside of it.

Annette shook her head. "I intend to find out."

## CHAPTER 23—JUDE

Monday morning, Beverly stopped Jude as she backed out of her driveway, her hand in the air and a smile across her face.

It was rare to find Beverly outside and smiling—and even rarer to be stopped—so Jude rolled her window down and waved and smiled back. "I read your article! Or *feature*!" Beverly neared Jude's car, so she went on, gushing. "It was terrific. You've got a great thing going, I think."

"Thanks," Beverly replied, and her expression turned more serious. "I hate to bug you on your way in to school—" Beverly stopped as if asking permission.

Jude waved her off. "I always go in way early. I have plenty of time." This was true. The radio clock in her car read six thirty. The real question was: Why was *Beverly* up and at 'em so early?

"I have an awkward favor to ask." Beverly leaned against Jude's car.

"As long as I'm not hunting for more dirt on high school teachers." She laughed, but Beverly didn't flinch. "Oh, wow. It's that parent complaint, isn't it? You want to know who the offending teacher is? The one who plays favorites?"

Beverly nodded. "Well, I think I already know. Word spreads like fire. What I'm curious about is what in the world *he* has to do with my cousin Forrest Jericho. Because Forrest is dead set on peeling the layers off of some scandal at the high school. This teacher must be at the center of it. Forrest won't come out with it, though. It's like he knows something, and he wants it to come out, but he doesn't want to be the one to come out with it." She snorted. "Does that even make sense?"

"I guess I'm out of the loop," Jude said. "Who's the teacher in question?"

Beverly jutted her chin across the cul-de-sac. "Tad Beckett."

"Really?"

"I guess. I don't think Kayla had him. Or maybe she didn't take his class." Beverly looked thoughtful and, surprisingly, not that sad.

"You know, the kids sometimes complain about

other teachers. I usually shut it down. Maybe I'll tune in."

"That'd be helpful."

"Beverly, do you think this is *serious*?"

"I'm not sure," she answered. "But I intend to find out. If it's the last thing I do."

~

JUDE UNLOCKED her classroom door and shrugged off the camel-colored wool coat she'd worn inside. The weather was changing fast—mornings turning winter-cold now. She hung her coat in the shared office and shelved her lunchbox in the refrigerator. The last order of business in the office was to set the coffee. Sharing a full-size coffee maker with the English department felt intimate, and Jude enjoyed being the one to get the caffeine percolating first. It made her feel a bit motherly. She was the oldest in the department, anyway. The other three teachers had to be under forty. They surely acted it—not in a bad way. In an unseasoned way. In a way that told Jude they were still trying to be friendly with students. It was often the younger teachers who were comfortable in that friendly role. Never the ones north of forty or fifty or sixty. Once you were over the hill as a teacher, you went from potential confidante to grandmother. At least, in Jude's experience.

After stepping back into her classroom with a fresh cup of coffee, a knock came at the door.

She glanced at the clock on her wall. Quarter after seven. A full hour before school commenced. If it were a faculty member out there, they would use their own key to open it. Nobody seemed to mind barging in on one another around the campus. But if it were a student…

Sure enough, when Jude opened up, Viviana Fiorillo's face appeared in the doorway. Behind her, Elijah Best. The indomitable duo from her very own street. "Well, what a surprise." Jude had neither one of them in class.

"Hi, Mrs. Banks. Mr. Belinger is letting us do extended research for an assignment and it's due today by three." Vivi wasn't shy. "It's become sort of a community thing. Maybe you're familiar with the disappearance of Temperance Temper?" She didn't wait for Jude to reply. "Well, she went missing over two decades ago and our thesis was that her disappearance was in some way connected with the local community. You see, our project has gotten some attention from the mayor's youth council as well as the Harbor Hills town council. Even Detective Grange is sort of cheering us on."

"We're not amateur sleuths or anything," Elijah interjected. It may have been meant as a joke, but he wasn't smiling. In fact, Elijah's demeanor was a striking contrast to Vivi's. He slouched at the shoulders and didn't offer so much as a smile. Typical male student. Less comfortable with academia than his female counterpart. Even so, Jude privately liked Elijah a great deal. He was more serious than most boys his age—most men, even. And despite his attitude at the present, he was, overall, very respectful.

"You're not sleuths," she repeated, keeping her tone measured. "But you're trying to solve an old mystery?"

"Right. Like I said, it's for Mr. Belinger's class project. We were supposed to report on a question about our community. Some students investigated the case of the failed tax override from the last election cycle. Another group studied that department store—what was it called? Woolworth's. It wasn't in town, but Mr. Belinger let them do it, anyway. Did you know that *particular* store closed because of a women's strike?" Vivi rushed ahead. "Neither did I. *Anyway*, we came to a dead end in our project, but then we had a few new leads. At this point, we are just gathering any new scraps of information in case they can help us *really* narrow down our theory."

Jude took a deep breath, her mind racing back to when Belinger brought in this pair's presentation board. "What's your theory?"

"Well, our *original* theory was that Temperance was murdered and her body hidden somewhere around town. We identified three suspicious local families.

They will *all* sound familiar to you, of course. The Gillespies, the Jerichos, and the Carlsons."

Jude nodded like this was all new information. It wasn't, but she didn't know if Belinger had told the kids he'd shown her their presentation board. "Right, yes. Beverly's family. Dean's. And...Carl's? Your old next-door neighbor, huh?" She looked at Elijah.

He gave her a funny look back. "I guess. I never met the guy."

"That's why we came to you, though, Mrs. Banks—"

"It's Miz. I'm not married, and Banks is my maiden name."

Vivi held up her phone in one hand. "May I ask your married name?"

But Elijah answered before Jude could. "It was Carmichael."

The girl tapped furiously into her device. "Carmichael. Okay. Are they from here? The Carmichaels?"

"The Carmichaels? My ex-husband's family?" Jude shook her head. "No."

Vivi didn't so much as glance up. She tapped again. "Oh. And you're not from here." It wasn't a question, but Jude gave her an affirmative nod of the head.

"Born in the greater Detroit area. Rochester Hills."

"Well, is it okay if we ask you some questions about Apple Hill Lane?"

Jude stiffened. "I don't know much about Apple Hill Lane. When we bought the house, we weren't here all that much." She looked to Elijah for help. "I'm sure you know this. We traveled. It's only this past summer I began to live here full-time."

"Well, maybe you heard something that you don't even realize—"

Jude held up her hand. "Sorry, Viviana. Maybe you could be more specific? I hate to shut you down, but I have sixty essays to grade this morning." She turned on a heel to head for her desk, where those very essays waited.

The two kids followed her in, letting the door close behind them.

"Oh, right. *Sorry*." Vivi didn't sound very sorry. "Anyway, I guess my *specific* question is—have you ever seen her?"

"Seen who?"

"Temperance Temper."

Jude raised her eyebrows as she lowered into her desk chair. "Oh. Well, I guess I'm not sure." Was Belinger *allowed* to have shared students' work? This felt like a big, fat catch-22. If she said yes, she'd seen the picture on their presentation board, could Belinger be in trouble? Could *she* be in trouble? If she said no but Vivi and Elijah already knew or found out that Jude *had* seen their board...then she'd be caught in a lie. A true lose-lose. "Um." She pretended to think.

Then she pretended the essay on top of her stack caught her attention. She selected a single red pen and held it to the paper. "Maybe. Yes, actually. I'm sure I've seen a picture of her." There. A semi-truth.

Vivi turned her phone to face Jude. "This is Temperance when she was young." Without turning the screen back to herself, she swiped. "And this is her just before she went missing."

A spark ignited in Jude's mind. A memory. Fleeting and ugly. Unattached to Belinger's show-and-tell.

"I've seen what she looks like, yes."

Vivi retracted the phone. "Did you ever see her on our street?"

Jude set her jaw. "Do you have evidence that she... visited Apple Hill?" Jude blinked. "Or something like that?"

A sigh lifted the girl's lithe body, and she frowned at her assistant, who shrugged in return. "Maybe."

Returning to the essay, Jude made a couple of swift proofreader's marks. *Capitalize proper nouns. Underline the titles of long-form works if handwritten.* She adjusted her glasses. "Like I said, dear, I simply haven't been around these last two decades. This year is the *first* one wherein I've lived on Apple Hill full-time." Jude was a broken record, and annoyance was setting in. Another question sprang to mind, but she framed it as a reminder. "You mentioned the Jerichos were on your short list of suspects."

Vivi's eyes flashed at her. "You know them."

"Everyone knows them," Elijah muttered, his gaze downcast like he was embarrassed now. Maybe he was.

"Dean is doing my pony wall." It came out pathetically. Jude tightened her grip on her pen and scrawled out *Vague* to the right of the topic sentence of paragraph number two. The irony in her feedback didn't escape her, but that was one of the small joys of grading essays. Those inside jokes with Jude and herself. *Vague topic sentence, and therefore a vague comment for you to see just what "vague" feels like!*

"Forrest is my mom's boss." Vivi was scrolling through her phone again.

"I know them, too." Elijah's face lifted, like he had something to contribute, even if it was just a small-town connection.

"Okay, so the reason we suspected the Jerichos was because of a falling out from around the time of Temperance's disappearance."

Jude set her pen down. Images of Dean came to mind. His no-nonsense demeanor. Sinewy arms. Long fingers. Strong hands. A mix of butterflies and spiders tickled her stomach. "What falling out?"

"Way, *way* back in the day, there was a Jericho who married a Temper. In Birch Harbor. It was, like, an old-timey thing where a dad didn't agree with it."

"Dead end," Elijah added vacantly. Another shrug.

Jude found her stomach settling at once, like a hole

along the beach, dug by some careless child, refilled with the flow of the tide, pushing new sand in like there was never a hole to begin with. She pushed aside the essays and propped her elbows on the center of her desk, resting her chin in her hands. "So that leaves two, then. The Carlsons and the Gillespies?"

"Right, but we have no way to learn about the Carlsons. From what we can tell, Carl had no children. Frankly, he had no *nothing*. There's nothing to be found. So, we're relying on locals to help fill in the gaps."

Jude had an idea. "Why not start with the Gillespies, then? Maybe you'll find something there."

## CHAPTER 24—BEVERLY

Beverly went into the office early, right after she talked with Jude. She planned to knock out some of the emails that continued to pour into her work inbox. Lots of new questions. Some affirmations from yesterday's column. Some complaints. But she knew the teacher question was a biggie because of how many similar questions rolled in. Questions and agreements. After she made some progress with correspondence, she turned her attention to her phone, planning to shoot off a message to Darry. *Can I swing by?*

Before she could set her phone back on her desk, it chimed.

Excited that he had replied so quickly, Beverly snatched it back, but the text wasn't from Darry.

It was an email from her mother. Just a subject line. No body or attachments. None of that surprised her.

Her mother's words were unexpected, however. *How do I forward an email?*

Instead of emailing back, Beverly called her. "What email? And to whom?" she asked once Bertie answered the phone.

"I got an email from Quinn's daughter, Vivi. She had a whole slew of questions about that poor missing woman, Temperance Temper. You know I knew them, right, Bev?"

Beverly frowned. "The Tempers?" She wasn't interested in this conversation right now. Sure, she'd love to crack the Temper case, but more urgent was the fact that over a dozen high school parents were complaining about a teacher and Darry Ruthenberg was ignoring every last one of them.

"Well, they're Birch Harbor people, but that one—way, *way* back when—she married a Jericho boy. It was a whole scandal."

"Did anything come of it?" Beverly asked, putting the phone on speaker and willing Darry to write her back right now so she could end the call and get down to business.

"No," her mother answered firmly. "It was just bad blood for a while, I think. The Jericho boy was my cousin. Forrest's uncle. Seems like that whole family is nothing but boys."

"I know. I always wanted a girl cousin."

"Sure, sure. That was another part of the issue, you know. So few girls came out of that family. Just boy after boy after boy. My aunts were so jealous of my mother. And then my cousins were so jealous of me for having you. Jealousy is a loathsome, dangerous thing, Bev."

Her mother's inflated language didn't scare Beverly. "So, what are you going to tell Vivi?"

"Just that," Bertie answered. "Other than the one unsupported marriage, there's nothing to share. Not about the Jerichos, and not about my dad's side of the family, either. I'm not sure where she got the idea that the boring old Gillespies have anything to hide. I wish we did, some days."

"Well, why do you need to forward anything, then, Mom? You can just hit Reply to Vivi's email and tell her that."

"Oh, well, I figured you'd want to know."

"Know what?"

"That she's rooting around in local history. Sort of like you did."

"I already knew about it. Vivi came to me first. She figured I knew more than I did. Or do." A new message flashed at the top of Beverly's screen. "Mom, I gotta go."

Darry hadn't exactly *invited* Beverly to his office, but when she told him she'd like to stop by, he didn't say no.

He didn't say yes, either.

"Mr. Ruthenberg is in a district administration meeting," Elaine, the secretary, informed Beverly. "Would you like to wait for him?"

Ah, so his meeting wasn't made up. "Actually, if it's fine by you, can I visit a couple of classrooms?"

"Oh," Elaine replied primly. "Um. I don't know. On what business?"

Beverly wasn't sure if she ought to flash her press credentials or if that would have the opposite effect of providing a good reason to be at the school. "I mean Jude Banks. Can I visit her? We're good friends. Just while I'm waiting for Darry?" Beverly gave her most earnest polite face.

It worked.

But just as she was turning down the hall to head to the English department, Darry appeared from the stairwell that led to the district offices above. Because classes were in session, the whole area was empty, save for the two of them. He wore a shirt and tie, slacks, and shiny, black shoes. His hair was done neatly, and he looked every bit the part of the principal. Nothing like the boyfriend Beverly knew once upon a time.

"Hi," she said, forgetting, for the moment, exactly why she wanted to talk to him.

"You're here." He took her by the shoulders. "Can we talk?"

"Well, yeah." She smiled. "I told you I was coming to see you. I figured we'd talk." Her sarcasm passed through him, and he pulled her out through the front doors and into the cool morning. "Where are we going?" she asked when he looked both ways to cross the street. The only place *to* go in this direction was the cemetery. Beverly did not want to go to the cemetery, and surely Darry should know this.

His answer came from a point of his finger.

Up the road, past the cemetery, stood a little corner deli that Beverly had always figured was out of business. But when they arrived there, they found a smiling older man behind the window. Darry ordered two coffees, and they took them to a little bench toward the back of the deli property. "Listen, Bev," he said, warming his hands around the paper mug. "I know you want to talk about the teacher complaint." His gaze stayed down, and she followed it to his hands. Nothing like Tom's hands. Beverly had often thought of her late husband as having a sort of effeminate build. Hips wider than his waist. Soft skin. Still, he was objectively handsome, just...in a pretty way. Darry wasn't pretty. He did woodworking on the weekends. Changed his own tires and oil. Raked leaves and did all his own home repairs. Beverly knew this because that's how Mr. Ruthenberg, Darry's father, had been. And Darry's hands proved as much. Rough and knobby. Somehow sexy, maybe.

"I just worry that you're not taking it seriously. I mean—I've never thought anything bad about Tad Beckett. And this is the first time I've heard about anything bad. Now that I'm running this column, I feel like certain things…well, I have to follow up. That's all. And I'm curious, Dar. Why leave it alone?"

"I can't tell you whether I'm leaving it alone, Bev. For all you know, I'm handling it."

She involuntarily reached for her satchel where her notepad lay in wait. "So, you *are* questioning him?"

Darry gave her a wary look. "Am I on the record?"

Beverly flushed and froze then let the satchel slide back to the ground. "No. Sorry."

"Look, I've already told you why I wasn't about to make a big deal. We were down this road years ago with another teacher, Bev."

"I know," she shot back. "And I plan to ask him about that, too—"

"Why?"

She returned a blank look. "Why what?"

"Why would you ask the other teacher about what happened? And dredge up a painful part of his history like that?"

"I—"

"The children. Everyone wants to protect the children." His tone was wry. "I get it. But that was a false allegation, and false allegations, Bev, can be as serious as—"

"As inappropriate teacher conduct?" She gave him a steely look. "I just want to show you one of the emails I got, Darry. Then I'll be out of your hair. I won't write about it. Even if it comes to something, I'll leave the school alone. You have my word. But you have to see this."

He unfolded the printout she handed him, and Beverly watched him read it, knowing exactly what he was seeing.

*Dear Beverly,*

*I am so excited to see your new column. Excited and a little nervous, though. Or maybe I'm just nervous to write to you like this. I know I'm rarely around. Anyway, I read the poor mother's complaint about a teacher who plays favorites. In fact, a few years ago, when my girls were at Hills High, we had a similar situation. The then-principal, Dwyer was his name, handled it abysmally. The truth was hidden in layers upon layers of gossip. The wrong teacher came under heat, probably because he was more attractive than the real culprit. Well, by then, all the accusers clammed right up. They saw that their claims cost someone his job, and all the while the real creep was freely preying.*

*The real creep was a new teacher. This will sound like another layer of gossip, probably, but around the time of this scandal, word had it that this young teacher had fathered the child of one of his students from another town. The girl was eighteen years old—age of majority. No one knows what became of that child, except that the father got off scot-free and turned his sights on another small-town school.*

*Well, I'll tell you the name of that teacher now, just so that Hills High can avoid another sordid scandal.*

*You'll want to pass this along to the current principal—I believe it's a Ruthenberg? Anyway, the teacher in question is Theodore Beckett.*

*I hope this is useful information and not alarming, Beverly. And I hope you're all well. I'll be back in town for the holidays. God bless you.*

*—Shamaine Lavigne, Apple Hill Lane.*

Darry looked up from the page. "Are you kidding me?" he whispered.

Beverly felt sick. She shook her head. "I'm not saying he's done anything, Darry. And neither is Shamaine. We're just saying that you need to take this more seriously."

"Promise me you'll convince Forrest to leave the story alone, Bev. Promise me you won't run any more of these so-called Q&As or Dear Abbys. Whatever they are. Not until I get this under control."

Beverly swallowed. She couldn't promise that. After

all, wasn't this a good thing? And no truly bad press? Just some emails of concern. They'd headed it off, hadn't they?

"I'm going to continue the column, Darry. At least for a little while. It's a good column." She felt her breath coming quicker. Panic was setting in.

"Bev, if this thing gets out before I can deal with it, I could lose my job." His eyes pled with her, and bile rose up in her throat.

It shouldn't be Beverly's problem, so there was no reason she should feel so personally connected to the whole thing. She blinked and chewed her lower lip and held Darry's gaze. Then it occurred to her. Why she cared about this column—why she cared about Darry's request. Why she cared about *anything*, for goodness' sake. Because she cared about *him*. "Listen," she began, running her tongue over her bottom lip and zipping her coat to her chin. "I haven't told anyone else this yet, but...I'm only going to run the column for another month or so, anyway."

"Oh." He looked hopeful. "Okay, then. So, you won't write about it, then?"

She shook her head. "No. Not as long as you handle it."

Darry's entire body relaxed. They stood together and started walking back to the school in silence.

Beverly allowed her gaze to drift through the cemetery gates and up toward her daughter's plot. She was glad Kayla had had Elijah. Something deep inside told her that he'd been something of a protector. Keeping her heart from being broken. Ironic, really. Beverly could use someone like that right about now.

They crossed the street, but before Darry went back inside, he caught her off guard by pulling her into a hug.

Beverly, who'd become used to carrying a stiff, angry body around for so long, gave in to the embrace, hugging him back and burying her face in his shoulder.

"Thanks, Bev," Darry whispered.

She nodded, squeezing her eyes shut. She wasn't sad over Darry, no. She wasn't sad about creepy Tad Beckett or even, honestly, his playing favorites. And she wasn't sad about Kayla—well, not right *then* at that very moment, at least.

Darry must have heard her quiet tears or sensed her insides go to mush, because he pulled back. "What's wrong?"

Shaking her head, Beverly ran a hand across her face and managed a smile. "Nothing. Nothing at all. Thanks for meeting with me and listening to what I had to say. You're a good friend, Darry."

She started to go, but just a yard into her journey back to the parking lot, Darry called, "Bev, wait." He took a long stride toward her, his expression unreadable.

"Yeah?" Hope welled up inside her, and she let it. No reason to squash a good thing these days. And hope, as a feeling, was a good thing. Even if whatever she had hope for...never came to fruition.

"How come you're not going to run the column for a longer time?"

She let a beat pass before gulping down the pesky nausea that came with big revelations. "I'm moving."

## CHAPTER 25—QUINN

Quinn had already scheduled her posts for the recent feature; now she was in charge of keeping up with comments. This was a more demanding task than one might think, especially once one particular share of the feature went viral. A reporter out of Birch Harbor was excited to exploit the fact that there was *trouble in a little paradise called Harbor Hills*, and Forrest felt damage control was in order.

"This wasn't supposed to backfire."

"Haven't you heard?" Quinn told him as they pored through a series of comments together. "No press is bad press."

"All press is good press," he corrected.

"Same difference."

"That's an oxymoron."

She grinned to herself. Their little rhetorical back-and-forth had become playful and even a bit flirty. Sitting in his office was now comfortable, not anxiety-producing, and Quinn even felt herself engaging in her compulsions less often when she was at work.

"So, what about the school feature?" Forrest asked, switching topics once they'd responded to a majority of the social comments.

"The school feature? You mean the angry parent?" Her fingers flew together beneath the edge of his desk, out of his sight. Her knee started bouncing. "I'm a little worried about it, too. Beverly hasn't gotten back to me, but she was supposed to go see Darry Ruthenberg this morning to get more information." She blinked then grabbed her bag from the floor, diving her hand in to retrieve her phone. "I'll text her a follow-up."

"It was a matter of time before something happened," Forrest said. It felt like a bit of a veiled comment, meant to tug out her curiosity. And it did.

"A matter of time before what?"

His freckles looked darker suddenly. She noticed this about him when he turned serious.

Quinn could be good at being quiet, so that's just what she did.

It worked.

Forrest laced his fingers on top of his desk and leaned in. "Listen, Quinn. You should hear about this from me before this whole story blows up."

"Okay." She kept her answers short. Quick. Her ears and eyes open. And her heart, too.

"Before I started working here, I was a teacher."

This was news, so to speak. She simply nodded and kept her face as impassive as she possibly could, even though her knee bobbed furiously below.

"There were these rumors going around—teenage girls and their crushes. You know. I guess I was a target for that. I was younger. Better looking back then."

Quinn couldn't help but raise an eyebrow. The flirting was becoming part of how they communicated.

He smirked. "Yeah, well, I mean—it's just part of life. Crushes. Right?" He gave her a hard look. "Did you have a crush on a teacher? I know I did. My eighth-grade science teacher."

Smiling, Quinn replied, "Yep. I had it bad for Mr. Powell, my freshman algebra teacher." He had been a redhead, too, but she kept that part private.

"Right, okay. You get it, then. Well, things got confused, then there was this secondary rumor about one of the new teachers getting into hot water up in Detroit. A senior from his old school got pregnant, and more rumors flew. The thing was, before that guy got pulled into the current at Hills High, a witch hunt had already broken out. The heat was on. One particularly nasty mother showed up to a board meeting. Called me a pervert because her daughter had talked about me." His jaw clenched and unclenched in time with his fists on top of the desk. "In the end, I quit."

She had no idea how to respond, and it likely showed.

He pressed his mouth into a tight line and just stared at her for a moment until his face turned into a grimace. "Is this a dealbreaker?"

"Dealbreaker?" Quinn's face fell. *Dealbreaker* was a loaded word. What was the deal? Their arrangement as boss and employee? Their relationship as...friends? *Were* they friends? Or—was it...could it be...?

He fumbled to reply. "I just mean—I hope you don't think less of me. It goes without saying, but I wasn't the pervert. The other guy was. Maybe he still is. That's why I've had a chip on my shoulder about the high school for so long." He frowned. "Do you?"

"Do I what?"

"Think less of me?"

Quinn shook her head immediately. "Of course not. Sheesh. I think *more* of you if anything—" She cringed. *She thought more of him because he was accused of indecent conduct as a teacher? What!?* "I just mean—it's wrong that it happened to you. I'd want the truth to come out, too. I do right now. I have a daughter there, for heaven's sake."

"That's why I got a little excited for Beverly to do an exposé. I don't know if she told you that I was pressuring her. It was rotten of me, it's just—I never knew who the other guy was. By the time I quit, everything went dark on it, like someone came into the school and threatened everybody to shut up."

"Rumors can be dangerous," Quinn agreed. "They can help the real bad guys fall through the cracks."

"They can ruin people's lives."

"Is that why"—she was careful with her words here —"Landon doesn't live with you?"

Forrest gave her a somber look. "Yeah. He was little when it happened, but once he found out, he was uncomfortable for a while. None of his friends knew or know, but he wanted that distance."

"What about his mom? Did she get weirded out, too?" Quinn thought about Matt and how he'd been nothing but supportive of her and Vivi both. She hadn't deserved him, probably.

"Nah. I didn't marry Julie, so there wasn't a whole lot of love lost there. She knows I'm not a pervert, anyway. I'm more of a geek than anything else." He laughed softly. "Julie is the one who got me this job, actually. It's her old position. She wanted to move on to blogging and new-age internet stuff. If I went from teaching to running the paper, then her child support would get a bump, so it worked out."

Quinn appreciated how frank Forrest was, but she also felt a little awkward getting such an intimate view of his personal life.

"Anyway, there you have it. The skeleton in my closet."

She smiled at him. "If that's the worst you've got, then I'd say you've lived a pretty tame life."

"I think that's why I love my job now. I get to live vicariously through the news."

"Speaking of the news," Quinn said, "do you think whoever that teacher was back then is the teacher indicated in Beverly's feature?"

He looked thoughtful. "That was my gut reaction, yeah. But if it's who I *think* it is, then I know him, and he's harmless. Not the sort of guy I'd be buddies with, but ultimately just another average Joe. Even if he were wicked enough to consider crossing a line, he's not that dumb. All eyes are on him and maybe they have been since back then. Sure, he might kiss up to the girls, but no way would he take it to the next level. Trust me when I say he's a wuss. He doesn't want that kind of attention."

Quinn found herself believing this. Clinging to it, even. The hope that school was a safe place for Vivi. That there were no predators there. That there'd be no conflict. Not after the last couple of years that girl had had. She made a mental note to follow up with Beverly and Annette and even Jude as soon as possible, but for now, she followed a piece of advice she'd once read in an online article about debilitating OCD. *Make a plan, then give yourself permission to not worry until your next actionable step*. Quinn's next actionable step wouldn't happen until after the workday, so for now, she settled back in her chair and popped over to a different one of her social media posts and its accompanying comments.

"Let's take a look at the Talkable post," she suggested.

They must have landed on the same post and same comment at the same exact moment because they laughed in tandem.

"Are you reading this, too?" he asked, swiveling his computer monitor for her to see.

*I agree with the first question! This town has nothing fun going on. I don't even know where to take my date on a Saturday night! Who's going to step up and make magic happen, Harbor Hills?*

Quinn smiled and shook her head. "Maybe *he* should step up and make magic happen, if he's so worried about a creative date idea."

Forrest blew air through his lips. "If I had a date, I know exactly where I'd take her."

Their eyes locked. Quinn rummaged in her brain for a non-oddball response, but nothing came. Instead, she just murmured, "Oh, really?"

Forrest licked his lips and fidgeted his hands on the top of his desk. His eyes fell away toward the window that looked out on the rest of the office. "If you want, I could show you."

"Are you asking me on a date?" Quinn hadn't realized she had the courage to ask him so bluntly. But there it was, the question hanging in the air between them like the preface to a kiss. She started to stutter a retraction, a take-back. Surely, he did *not* mean to ask her on a date, but then—

"Yes."

~

VIVI ARRIVED home that afternoon defeated.

Quinn, on the other hand, was floating on cloud nine. She and Forrest had made plans for that coming weekend, and the rest of the workday had been a deliciously uncomfortable blur of flirting and work, work and flirting.

"Eli thinks it's not worth it," Vivi admitted, after sinking into a chair at the kitchen table.

Quinn passed her a plate of gingersnap cookies and a glass of milk.

"What's this?" Vivi asked.

"Your after-school snack. I was feeling inspired." Quinn sat in the chair across from her daughter and leaned forward. "Do you mean he thinks the extra credit isn't worth it?" The poor thing. Vivi had become obsessed with the Temperance Temper project and how many extra points she could squeeze out of that teacher.

"Yeah. We heard back from Mrs. Gillespie at the bed-and-breakfast, and there's nothing she knows about her family that might mean something for the Temper case. She said all there was to her dad's side of the family was obesity and a cigar scandal from the '90s when her grandpa smuggled a Cuban across the border."

Quinn laughed but then gave her daughter a sympathetic look. "Did she have any other info?"

"Well, we asked her about the Jericho side of her family since that's her mom's side. There was a little more drama—jealousies, mainly. A bit of a fight over the bed-and-breakfast. That was it."

"Well, you still have the Carlsons to work with, then, right? Maybe the Carlsons are your main suspects."

Vivi looked irritated. "Yeah, but there is literally no Carlson around to talk to, and no one here even knows them. And anyway, like, Mrs. Gillespie said they were just normal people from what she knew. Maybe arrogant. Not a lot of kids in the family, I guess? But she thought they did have that one descendent, that girl she'd talked about. Doesn't matter, though, because Mrs. Gillespie says that the girl never even lived here, anyway."

"Maybe," Quinn replied, "you should track down this so-called girl. Find out what *she* has to say."

Giving Quinn a hard look, Vivi's face twisted thoughtfully. "I don't even know if she's alive."

"Why should she be dead?" Quinn answered. "She's probably not much older than me. Right? If she was a girl in the, what, seventies? Then she'd be fifty or sixty by now. Right?"

"Well," Vivi replied, her expression revealing a nervousness in her daughter that Quinn had rarely been witness to. "Let's just say...I know about an unidentified dead person." She gulped. "Here. On Apple Hill."

## CHAPTER 26—ANNETTE

Come Tuesday morning, when she *still* hadn't heard back from Tad Beckett, Annette asked Roman if they ought to call the police. Up to now, they'd gone back and forth and back and forth. First, Annette had said *not* to call and Roman had said they'd *better* call. Then they flipped. Then they flipped back. And back again.

"It's not our house anymore, Annie," Roman said as they sat on the back porch, staring off into the yard. "Should we involve ourselves at this point? Especially with what we're about to do?" Their new plan was in the works, but as of now, nothing big had happened quite yet. They were still Best on the Block Realty. Still living in the red cottage together. Still parenting a teenager who was about to be out of their house.

Maybe for good. Those darn changes couldn't come soon enough.

"We *found* the body, though. What if we get in trouble for *not* reporting this, Roman?" She took a long pull of her wine—store brand Riesling. Annette didn't even know there were such things as generic adult beverages. It was the best they could afford lately, and it got the job done. Hopefully, she'd move up a shelf within the next couple of months, though. If all went according to plan.

Roman pointed across the yard to the far-back stretch of property. On Dogwood, people didn't have fences, really. There were fences at the backs of all the properties along that street because Apple Hill yards had fences. But Dogwood yards did not have fences. They were rolling hills of grass sweeping around scant orchards of pine and oak trees until that grass rolled right under the fence of the neighbor behind. Quinn's backyard. Annette's, Shamaine's in the corner lot across the street, then beyond and to the forest at the east of town.

"Have you seen that?" Roman pointed with his margarita glass.

"What?" she asked, downing the last of her wine and squinting into the darkening distance.

"The backyard cemetery."

A laugh bubbled up from her chest. "That's right," she said, entirely amused and floating from her drink.

She glanced at Roman. "That's the Carlson family plot, remember?" She stood up and smoothed the butt of her yoga pants, feeling her hands move over her granny panty lines. Soon enough, she'd get to wear yoga pants every day. Not with granny panties underneath. But yoga pants, all the same. *If* the plan worked out.

"Yeah. I knew you *knew*. I just didn't know if you'd taken a look." There was an edge to his voice, and she turned and gave him a look.

"*No*," Annette answered, matching his tone. "I was sort of hoping we wouldn't be around long enough for it to matter."

Roman grunted behind her, and she turned to see him following her across the grass, his hands tucked into his pockets and his glasses glinting with the orange glow of the sunset. "It was just a house, Annette. No different than this one. It's up to *you* to make a home, you know."

"It's more than that, Roman." She took a breath before launching into the very monologue she had been over in her head time and again. "Apple Hill Lane —that was our first house together. It was Elijah's first house. His only house, until now. I've made friends on that street, and I know—we are just behind them now. Maybe even closer to Quinn's house, but it's *different*. I can't look out my kitchen window and see Jude fussing with her burning bush. I can't call upstairs for Elijah to turn the music down. In this house, it's like he *knows* he can't be loud. He hasn't played music one single time. The move knocked the spirit from him. I'm sure of it. And entertaining—*Roman*, you *know* what it meant to me to entertain year-round. This house is adorable. But, Roman, it has *none* of that. So, sure. Both are houses. Both *can* be homes. But I belong over there."

"I know."

She whipped her head to him. "You know?"

"I don't like that we're here and the Becketts are there any more than you do, Annie."

"You don't?"

"Well, geez, Annie, *no*. This whole thing is a mess. Do you think this is how I saw my life going?" He gave her a disappointed look. "Obviously not."

"Isn't this your chance to tell me I can only grow if I accept this change and, I don't know, *roll* with it or something?" She laughed mirthlessly, but Roman grabbed her hand and swung her around to him.

"I could say that. I could say that everything happens for a reason. Or a cliché like coal turning to diamonds under pressure or you can't grow if you don't change."

"You could," she agreed. He released her hand and folded his arms over his chest.

"But I won't."

"Why not?" Annette felt desperate to hear Roman's

answer. She wanted to shake some sense into him. She wanted him to tell her that she would be fine. *They* would fine. That this whole move would make everyone better in the end.

But he didn't. Like he said he wouldn't.

"Why can't you tell me that, Roman?" Annette pressed.

"Because sometimes, it's just not true." His mouth drew up in a half smile, and Annette felt more confused than ever. Confused about their *plan*. Confused about living in the red cottage that was so adorable but so not *her*. Confused.

And for now, she'd just have to stay that way. And that was okay. Sometimes, sitting with confusion was the only way to work through it. The only way to learn.

THEY FOUND themselves at the lip of their property line. A crooked row of sunken stone markers ran almost the entire width of their yard. Such an oddity. "It's weird, isn't it?"

"That there's a cemetery in suburban Michigan?" He chortled. "Yeah, but Harbor Hills used to be all forest and farmland. From Birch Harbor clear on to Detroit. My grandparents farmed just north of here. They had their own family cemetery, too. All rural areas did, I think. That's what I've heard, anyway."

"Is that where you want to be buried? In the Best family cemetery north of town?" She meant it snarkily, but actually, it was as serious a question as any. She and Roman had never had that sort of conversation. Seemed too morbid. Maybe now was a good time to find out, though. It'd be important for her to relay that to Elijah one day. And vice versa in case she made it out of life before Roman did.

"My parents have eight plots in Birch Harbor, actually. But I've never thought much about it. I guess I figured we'd just stay here, so to speak." He looked at her from the corner of his eye. "Don't tell me you already bought one."

She chuckled and squatted down to the marker nearest her feet, then cleared away some of the weedy grass. "No. No, I may be organized and fanciful, but not *that* organized and fanciful. So, don't worry, Ro—you won't be stuck with me in the afterlife if you don't want to be."

"Well, isn't this funny!" A cry came from beyond the fence. Annette shot up and scanned the area.

Elora Beckett, her face full and shiny, appeared over top of the wooden pickets.

"Hi!" Annette cheered in response. "It's like an alternate reality or something," she joked of their flip-flopped circumstances.

"Yeah." Elora wasn't smiling. Not frowning, either. In fact, she looked like she was searching for something. "Actually, it's not so coincidental this time." She said it like it was a confession.

Roman, ever the people-pleaser, made a joke in reply. "What, no dog poop out there yet?"

"No." Elora stole a glance back toward the house. "It's been hard. The move."

Annette walked nearer to her. "Moving is hard. Especially with a little one and in *your* condition. I don't know how you're managing."

"I don't, either. It's, well, like I said. It's been hard."

"Elora," Annette said, tired of waiting on this. "Have you two gotten in touch with the authorities yet? Regarding the body, I mean. It's been over two weeks now, but we haven't noticed anyone come by. We haven't had anyone over here to question us. We're wondering if something is wrong." She meant every word, every sympathetic, nosey little word. Annette was feeling antsy about the lack of reporting. It felt wrong. Not just because it coulda, shoulda, woulda been a ploy to get the Becketts out of her house, but because, well, it was a skeleton. There was no gray area here. Even if it was an old burial site like the ones she and Roman had just examined. It was *wrong* not to tell somebody. And even worse, Annette made the mistake of Googling what to do if you found human remains on your property.

You were supposed to call the police. Right away.

It was an even bigger deal than either she or

Roman had realized.

Roman joined the two women at the corner of the yard. "I'm happy to make the call, Elora. To the sheriff's office or the local police—whichever you prefer."

"Well, I've been asking Tad to do it, but with school, he's so busy. We're under a lot of stress, truth be told. We knew we wanted to upgrade—we needed a bigger house—but we're doing the math, and the bills here are going to be higher than we've been budgeting for." She pressed a hand to her head. "I'm oversharing. This is awful." She looked about to cry, and that's when Annette moved to the gate in Quinn's fence. Without hesitating, she opened it and crossed Quinn's yard over to her old yard. The Becketts' yard. Once there, she wrapped poor Elora in her arms, shushing her as she wept. "Is Tad home now?" Annette whispered as she eyed Roman over the fence.

Elora nodded. "He's inside," came her muffled voice. "With the baby." Elora was that sort of mom. Like Annette, who still called Elijah, even now all grown up, her baby. No matter his age, that's all Annette saw when she looked at him. Maybe she and Elora had more to share than each other's old homes.

"Mind if Roman goes and has a chat with him?" Though they hadn't planned this, it was growing patently clear that something was very, *very* wrong with the Beckett family situation. The least of which, in fact, was the skeleton in their backyard.

## CHAPTER 27—VIVI

Vivi's mom had tried calling Annette on the phone a few times, after Vivi explained everything. When Annette didn't answer, Vivi begged Quinn not to march over there.

"She'll be mad I told you."

"It's not her fault there are human remains, Viv. Maybe she needs advice, though. You can't just...*not* report that. Now that I know, I can't just *not* do anything."

"Mom," Vivi groaned. "Just—please wait. Let me text Eli. See what he says. Maybe Mrs. Best has a plan."

"Fine," her mother agreed. "Do the others know, though?"

"What others?"

"Jude? Beverly? Do they know there's a body there?"

Vivi shrugged. "I don't think so."

"And you believe it's that little girl Mrs. Gillespie has talked about. The one who used to visit Bernie Carlson."

"That's what Annette told me."

"Annette told you that? That she thinks it's that girl?"

"The bones were small. Not small like an animal or child. But, they seemed frail," Vivi confessed. She felt a lot like barfing just then. "Can we skip dinner tonight?"

Her mom started up with the blinking and finger tapping. Vivi felt bad for her. She couldn't cope under the best of circumstances. Now here she was, held hostage by Vivi's request to keep quiet. When what Quinn really needed was another adult. Someone to tell her it would be okay just as Quinn had told Vivi it would be okay.

Headlights washed over the front windows, and it occurred to Vivi that it was getting dark outside. Late. The headlights didn't pass like they normally would if it were a car driving up Crabtree Court. Instead, they intensified until they were shining directly into the parlor. "Who's that?"

"Oh." Quinn clicked her tongue. "I almost forgot." She pressed her hand to her hair, pushing it and pulling it, then dashed to the junk drawer beneath the microwave, rummaging until she came up with a lip gloss.

"Mom?" Vivi asked, confused as Quinn sloshed what seemed like half the tube over her mouth. She then grabbed Vivi's backpack from its slump on the floor, stuck her hand in the side pocket and exposed an almost-full pack of gum.

"How'd you know that was there?" Vivi accused.

"I'm the one who put it there," Quinn replied, tearing off the wrapper and shoving the stick into her mouth just in time for the doorbell to chime.

"I wondered who did that," Vivi muttered to herself, following her mom to the front door.

When Quinn opened it, Vivi was unsurprised to see Forrest Jericho standing outside.

"Everything okay?" he asked, looking concerned.

Quinn let out a sigh. "This is so awkward," she said. "I forgot that Annette said she'd call you. We're fine. Really. You don't need to be here."

"Why does he need to be here?" Vivi asked.

Quinn did a double take as if she'd forgotten her own daughter lived there. "Oh, Viv. It's just—with that weird complaint about Mr. Beckett, I was nervous. I told Annette, and she said she'd call in reinforcements." Her mom smiled at Forrest, and Vivi was proud of herself for not vomiting then and there. Both from talk of the human bones lying in the ground next door and her mother, coyly flirting with Landon's dad. Bleh.

"I'll camp out in the living room. It's no big deal."

"Really, Forrest. Go home. It's silly that I even said anything to Annette. I spoke with Beverly Castle this afternoon, and it sounds like everything with Tad is being handled."

Vivi gasped. "Are they firing Mr. Beckett?"

"No," Quinn answered. "I didn't say that. I said they are going to handle it."

"Oh my gosh, that's insane. I mean, I don't have his class, but I've definitely heard that he looks down girls' shirts."

"Viv," her mom hissed. "Go upstairs and get ready for dinner."

"We're skipping dinner, remember?"

Her mother was losing patience fast. "Fine," Vivi conceded and turned on her heel toward the staircase. She'd go upstairs. She'd call Eli. She'd get the *real* scoop.

At least, that was the plan.

Until a second pair of headlights streamed in through her bedroom window. Then a third. And a fourth.

And some of those headlights weren't headlights at all.

They were the flashing lights of police cars.

## CHAPTER 28—JUDE

It happened fast. The police tearing down the road. Beverly rushing across the cul-de-sac in her robe. Cop cars at odd angles in front of Annette's old house. The Becketts' *new* one.

Jude wanted to grab Liebchen and run far away from all this drama. But that would be much worse, ultimately. So instead, she pulled on her flannel poncho, scooped up her big, fluffy girl, tucked her feet into the galoshes sitting by the door and walked out to join the hysteria.

Everyone was there, at the Becketts' house, huddled in front.

Roman and Annette and Elijah. Quinn and Vivi. Beverly and her cousin Forrest, although he was hanging nearer to Quinn, oddly. Jude recalled they worked together, too. Elora and her young son, although they were on the porch, speaking with a police officer whose back was to the street. The only notable person missing was Mr. Beckett—Tad.

"What happened?" Jude asked Beverly when she joined their shivering group on the front lawn.

Annette broke from her brood to join Jude and Beverly. Soon, Quinn was there, too.

"Here's what I know," Annette began ominously. "When we were getting ready to move, we found human remains in the backyard." Before anyone could properly react, she put her hand out, splayed. "I *know*. It sounds bad. I figured it was one of those old graves, you know? They are everywhere here. This place was a rural farming community before we all barged in." The group murmured in an agreeable response. "Well, it was actually Elijah and Vivi who found them, and I was worried it'd upset the sale. I asked the kids to keep mum. It was stupid, I know. But we disclosed to the Becketts on the condition that they'd call the proper authorities."

"Annette," Beverly gasped. "You just...looked the other way? You kept it a secret? That's, like, *illegal*."

"They are very, very old, Bev." Annette's voice wobbled, even as she tried to sound reassuring. "Anyway, I know. It was stupid. Roman and I argued up and down over it. We've been freaked out, okay? And I admit, I thought maybe they'd be scared off." She glanced up toward the porch. "Please don't think I'm a selfish brat." Her eyes begged them, and Jude knew it was earnest. She knew how much Annette loved her home. How much she had dreaded moving. How it had shattered her world. "Anyway, when we realized Tad never made the call, we poked around. This was tonight, actually. Then Elora admitted he hadn't called, so we just...*did* it."

"Why didn't he call?" Quinn demanded. "Did he figure they were dog bones?"

"They *weren't* dog bones. But I'm not sure he ever looked, anyway." Annette's voice dropped an octave. "I think he didn't call because he didn't want any attention."

Beverly chimed in. "Makes perfect sense. He has a checkered past, right?"

"Right," Annette agreed.

"Oh my gosh," Quinn breathed. "Is he going to be arrested? Is he a *pedophile*?" Her eyes were wide with fright, but Jude knew better than to let things get so out of hand.

"Tad Beckett's not a pedophile. And he won't be arrested."

"How do you know?" Annette asked.

It was Beverly who answered. "She's right. Darry told me everything."

Quinn added, "Forrest told me everything, too."

"What do you two know?" Jude asked Quinn and Beverly.

They exchanged a look, and Beverly took the liberty of replying, explaining everything she knew about Tad Beckett possibly having an affair with an eighteen-year-old back at his old school. How his reputation preceded him here—how it was any wonder he never lost his teaching license. How he continued to let his eye wander but that, ultimately, he'd never crossed any serious boundary. Not at Hills High, rest assured.

"What happens next?" Jude asked, entranced by this web of deceit and intrigue.

Annette acted like she knew. "When Roman talked to the cops, they said they'd send down the county coroner and a police escort. Because we didn't report this in a timely fashion, I think they got a little worked up and sent down an extra unit. Roman explained everything to the detective, and we're off the hook." She let out a breath. "For now. But I don't think Tad is. They are probably asking him why he held off. I'm sure we're going to incur a fine at the very least. Maybe community service."

"Yikes." Quinn squeezed Annette's shoulder. "This is ridiculous."

The officer who'd been chatting with Elora moved down from the porch and stopped where the ladies were gathered.

"Hiya, Bev," he said, and even his voice had a comforting lilt to it.

Beverly lifted her hand to the other women. "Ladies, this is Detective Grange."

Once they introduced themselves, Jude petted Liebchen and tried her best to ignore it all.

Annette stole his attention. "What happens next, Detective?"

"It'll depend on a few factors," he said. "First of all, if the remains are older than your tenure in the home, you'll be cleared, I'm sure. I can't speak to Tad's delinquency in reporting. Maybe he didn't care. Seems like that guy isn't long for Harbor Hills, if ya ask me."

"Why?" Beverly asked.

"His wife said as much." He hooked a thumb up to the porch, where Elora now sat on Annette's porch swing, her young son nestled into her side. Her free arm supporting her belly. She looked to be a tragic mess, and Jude felt terrible for her. She needed help is what that woman needed. She needed sleep. She needed *friends*.

"She said they're leaving?" Annette asked.

He replied, "She said *he's* leaving. Apparently, there're some other problems in the marriage."

The women shared a knowing look.

Detective Grange went on. "Anyway, beyond that, they'll have to examine the remains and determine if they have forensic quality or not."

"What does that mean?" Beverly asked.

He answered, "If whoever died did so under foul circumstances."

"Oh." Jude clutched her throat. It sounded so *serious*. A little scary, too.

"There was no marker, apparently, and that makes it a little trickier. But we'll do our best to get an ID on the body soon. Maybe there's someone out there looking for answers."

"Maybe it's a Native American burial ground," Annette suggested.

"Doubtful," Detective Grange replied. "Lots of old graves out here. All farm country. We've got neighbors who've got a whole family in their backyard."

"You're right about the marker. There was nothing," Annette said. "We'd built Eli's fort in that exact spot. I can't believe Roman hadn't noticed it before, truth be told. Goes to show how he just poured some cement down and set about to building. Typical." She pursed her lips.

"Well, you'll have nothing to worry about, I'm sure. Best thing to do is answer your phone. I'll be in touch to process it all." He rested his hand on Beverly's shoulder. "In the meantime, you might want to reach out to Mrs. Beckett. She's gonna have a time of it, I think."

The detective took off, and the other three women began chattering about a plan to draw Elora into the fold, but Jude strode after the detective. "Mr. Grange" she called in the cold night. Liebchen purred in her arms, and she knew she looked like a nut, but right now they all looked like a bunch of nuts.

"Yes, ma'am?"

"What happens after you ID the remains?"

"What happens?" He scratched his head. "We return them to the family for a proper burial—assuming there's family alive still. Next of kin, you know."

"What if it's a forensic situation, like you said?"

"You mean a crime?" He shifted his weight evenly across both feet, squaring to her. "Do you think a crime took place here, ma'am?"

"Oh, no. No, I don't," Jude backpedaled quickly. "It's just—should we be *worried*?"

His stance and face softened. "Oh, no, ma'am. You ladies have nothing to worry about. Surely not here. Harbor Hills is the safest small town in America. People look out for each other here. They don't tolerate riffraff." He patted the gun holstered at his hip. "Anyway, if you ever need a thing, don't hesitate to call the station." With that, he winked and left.

And Jude would continue to wonder. Just how safe was her street? How safe were her neighbors?

But mostly she wondered what *else* were they going to discover on Apple Hill Lane?

## CHAPTER 29—ANNETTE

About a week later, the fog had lifted over Apple Hill Lane. With such strife streaking through her life and her friends' lives, it only made sense to Annette to plan a party, something harvest inspired. Something about change and newness and dried-out sunflowers and seeds. That whole thing.

The problem, however, was that she couldn't very well host a party in the little red cottage. Elora's house was out, too, because it was an active archeological dig site. Annette knew that Quinn was getting tired of hosting, so she didn't bother to ask.

Instead, she went to Jude. "Please? Your house is gorgeous. Don't you want to show off the work Dean did? The new paint job? The little construction project?"

But Jude was adamant. "I don't do parties anymore. Goodness, Annette, I don't even do *holidays* anymore."

"You don't do *holidays*?" Annette tsked. "Oh, Jude. You do, too. You're as Catholic as a nun. Heck, I thought you *were* a nun until very recently."

"Nuns can't get married." Jude was unamused. "And anyway, there's a difference between celebrating the holiday in vain and celebrating in earnest."

Her response was so somber and so melancholy that Annette realized she'd better keep an eye on ol' Jude Banks. But she wasn't going to apply any more pressure. Besides, she had one more person to ask.

"Beverly!" Annette cried when the blue front door swung open at Annette's unexpected visit. "I have a *huge* favor to ask you."

Beverly let her in and they sat as her two precious pups panted at their knees. "Bev, I want to host a party. Sort of a block party, but indoors. Wouldn't it be nice to get to know Elora a little better? Maybe Shamaine will come to town, even. Who knows?"

To Annette's great surprise, Beverly agreed.

~

THE EVENING of their harvest dinner, Annette had an ulterior motive. Sure, she wanted to welcome Elora to the street more formally. She wanted to celebrate

Beverly's big successes with the new feature and Quinn's contributions, too.

But more to the point, Annette and Roman had signed all their paperwork. The plan was in motion, and Annette would hate for her friends to find out about their new chapter from something like a gossip column.

Everyone arrived on time and looking beautifully festive. Not a single person was without a date, either. Eli came with Vivi—no, they hadn't solved their case yet, but *yes*, Belinger had granted them ample extra credit. They dressed like they usually did, and that was fitting enough. Both in warm flannel tops and jeans, with their gorgeous hair and faces—they could be models, Annette knew. Both of them. They'd make the most adorable babies, too, but she knew better than to say something like that out loud.

Beverly had invited Darry, although *only* as a friend, she'd said. Annette had her own suspicions about this, especially when the two seemed more like cohosts than anything else. Darry helped refill drinks and chips. Beverly sat close to him through appetizers, her dark red blouse in stark contrast to his Kelly-green polo. They looked like a Christmas package, wrapped together as two gifts sometimes are. The ribbon in this case, though, was an invisible thread between them. Something Annette would later learn was their history. High school sweethearts. High school sweethearts of the kind that never *really* moved on. Regardless of her insistence that it was purely platonic, Beverly otherwise seemed happy. Happy and a little bit mysterious. Like she had a little secret she was waiting to share.

Quinn brought Forrest, and they, too, made a striking couple. No, they weren't officially dating. However, Quinn had confessed they'd been on a few *real* dates. She'd even shared that Forrest had taken her on an official tour of Harbor Hills, stopping at every hotspot to show her the town. From Babe's Doughnuts for breakfast and coffee to the old, converted gas station out by the highway for lunch. The old-fashioned movie theater for a matinee. They went thrifting at the Penny House. Fishing out at Lake of the Hills. He'd even shown her the cherry orchard uptown. Everywhere that she'd never been, and she'd been glowing ever since. And tonight, she glowed, too. In a burnt-orange sweater that hung low on dark-wash jeans, she was stunning. The added height from her riding boots didn't seem to bother Forrest, who, at a smidgeon under six feet tall was effectively shorter than her. He looked dashing anyway, in a dark green sweater and jeans. His reddish waves gelled stylishly. And they smelled good, too.

Jude had refused to bring a date, but Beverly had managed to convince her not to leave when Dean arrived with Forrest. Jude had been on edge lately, acting like a nervous wreck over the whole mess from the Becketts' yard. Between that and the accusations of indecency against Tad, Annette could see that Jude was offended to be in such company. But she managed to lighten up for the evening. She even sat next to Dean, and they—funny enough—matched in black sweaters and khaki slacks. Jude's makeup was impeccable, though, and it was clear as day that Dean was enamored of the enigmatic single woman.

Then there was Elora, who was due so soon that she looked like she might explode. She had her son, Lincoln, who delighted in spending the evening out. In just the short time since the police incident, Tad had resigned from his position at the high school and moved back home with his parents at his wife's behest. Elora was picking up the pieces from her marriage gone bad, and Annette could see she was happy to be with a group of friends. Happy to be one of them, too. It was only a matter of time before Elora was as close to the four women as they had grown in just a short span of months. So, in a way, Elora had her son, yes, but she had them, too. The Apple Hill gang.

And for herself, well, Annette had Roman. Her husband.

And, she had an announcement to make. She clinked her fork against her glass of sherry—Jude's contribution to the dinner.

"Roman and I would like to share something," Annette said. Roman stood with her and looped his arm around her waist, right where she was carrying an extra ten pounds. An extra ten pounds that he said he loved. An extra ten pounds that she had decided she could live with.

"Ooh," Quinn teased. "Are you pregnant?"

Annette cackled and Roman tickled her ribs, and the group roared together in laughter at such a ridiculous thing. Eli and Vivi shrank in the corner, as teenagers do. When everyone settled down, Annette went on.

"When we moved onto Dogwood—and we love that street, by the way; we love the house too—but when we moved there, we knew we needed to make another change. That maybe we'd made the wrong change."

Roman took over for a beat. "We are lucky as they come. We've got Eli—a perfect son. We've got each other, most of all. But we realized we'd made a mistake somewhere along the way."

"That's right," Annette agreed. She glanced down at her own outfit. She'd thrown on a denim button-down over denim jeans that were comfy. She'd done her makeup and painted her nails fire engine red. She'd blown out her hair. She'd slipped into an ancient pair of sheepskin boots that were tragically out of style but also, somehow, timeless. She wasn't dolled up, but she felt like herself. She felt beautiful and cute and hip and like *herself*. "We tried to be the best," she went on, glancing at her husband, who squeezed her side gently, urging her ahead.

Annette nodded to Elijah, his cue to bring out the sign. He ducked into Beverly's kitchen and returned quickly, the sign facing him so no one could read it yet.

The group shared bewildered expressions, and Annette ate it all up.

"We've decided that we needed a change, all right. An overhaul, even," Roman announced.

"Gone is Best on the Block," Annette said, lifting her hand to her son, who flipped the sign around. "We'd like you to meet the new Realtors in town, everyone!"

All eyes turned on the sign, and Annette read it aloud, her heart thumping with excitement.

"The House around the Corner Realty. Because the perfect *home* doesn't have to be the best on the block. And in fact, it might be *just around the corner*."

# CHAPTER 30—QUINN

Quinn loved every moment of the harvest party. She loved that her best friend had a new mission and vision for her life. She loved that Elora was joining their ranks. She loved that she had Forrest to share it all with.

Mostly, though, she loved that Vivi was happier than Quinn had ever seen her. So happy, in fact, that Quinn started to get that feeling all over again. The dread. The sense of doom. The sense that something from the past was sure to come rearing its ugly head. Because that's how life worked. You had to take the good with the bad.

But maybe that was okay, because nowadays, Quinn didn't have to take the bad *alone*.

## CHAPTER 31—BEVERLY

Beverly was surprised that none of her neighbors noticed just how barren her house had become. She'd spent the past week slowly selling pieces off on Craigslist and MoveOn.-com. She'd gotten some packing done, too.

It was Darry who, at the party, recognized a change in the house. "It's really happening, isn't it?" he murmured when they had a moment alone in the kitchen.

"I can't stay here." She answered him flatly, her eyes down on the bread she was slicing. "Not in the house."

"What about in this town?" he prompted, willing her to look at him. She could feel his eyes.

Beverly looked. "Where would I go? I've been long since priced out of this town. The market is crazy here.

And anything that *is* for sale is too big. I want something small."

Darry grabbed her hands and squeezed them. "Beverly, I get it. I really do. But before you rush to get out of here, will you do me a favor?"

"What?" she asked.

"Don't do anything before the holidays."

"Why not?"

"Because I need a date to the Harbor Hills Christmas Gala."

# EPILOGUE

Over the ensuing few years, Grandad and the woman developed a routine, awkward as it may have been. The woman would go back to Apple Hill Lane some years on Easter, Thanksgiving, or for Christmas. Grandad would roast a ham or a turkey. She'd bake rolls and whip up sides. They'd eat on TV trays in front of the console television, a sporting event on mute on the small, square, bubbled screen.

After, she'd help tidy up, going so far as to make a dent in the hoard.

Eventually, an understanding had taken place. As though they were a little family, their routines grew refined, and the odd couple established these rudimentary family habits together. So, when the woman showed up for Thanksgiving on that particular year, she knew what to expect. She expected a little regression. That Grandad would look a tad older and the house a tad less kempt than when she'd been there the time before. He'd be a little crankier, and she'd be a little less patient with him.

They'd eat.

They'd watch football.

She'd clean, making no real strides toward progress.

She'd leave.

But on that particular Thursday afternoon, when she arrived at the curb with its overgrown grass and gradually encroaching spread of front-yard junk, a change whipped through the air.

She felt it as soon as she stepped out of her car. A nip—a twist and a *change*. Not in the seasons, no. But *there*. On Apple Hill Lane.

Different cars peppered the street, like those once-empty neighboring houses actually had *people* in them.

A new house had gone up, too, directly behind Grandad's. A red cottage that stuck out like a sore thumb against the colonials the Carlson family had had built over the decades. Amazing how quickly that sort of thing materialized. New homes ought to take years. Not months. Then again—had the red cottage been there at Easter? Or even the Christmas before? Suddenly, the woman wasn't so sure her memory was quite right.

But the difference she felt wasn't just the changes to the street, such that they may be. It was another change. A subdermal one, but a bigger one.

Writing off the feeling as general holiday anxiety, the woman gave her loose hair a shake and pushed up to the front door.

Now comfortable enough to rap once and twist the knob herself, she did just that, but the door gave way on its own.

She started to take a step in, stopping in her tracks when she met the gaze of the person who opened the door.

It was a stranger.

The stranger looked back into the innards of the house. "Carl! She's here!"

But the woman—who now felt like a girl all over again—was confused. Confused at the stranger and confused at the name.

Grandad's name was Bernard.

Not Carl.

***

*Finish the saga with* The House that Christmas Made.

## ALSO BY ELIZABETH BROMKE

Harbor Hills:

*The House on Apple Hill Lane (1)*

*The House with the Blue Front Door (2)*

*The House around the Corner (3)*

*The House that Christmas Made (4)*

Heirloom Island

Birch Harbor

Hickory Grove

Gull's Landing

Maplewood

## ABOUT THE AUTHOR

Elizabeth Bromke writes women's fiction and contemporary romance. She lives in the mountains of northern Arizona with her husband, son, and their sweet dogs, Winnie and Tuesday.

Learn more about the author by visiting her website at elizabethbromke.com.

# ACKNOWLEDGMENTS

Elise Griffin, Beth Attwood, Tandy Oschadleus—thank you for helping polish my stories! They are better because of you. Thank you! Also, I am also grateful to my incredible advance reader team. Your support is invaluable to me. Thank you for reading my books and helping me share them with the world.

My appreciation goes out to several helpful early readers and sources of encouragement, especially Jeanie and Tisa. You are both such wonderful friends. Tisa, we'll miss you! For my other neighbors, who are equally wonderful and supportive, especially Janice, Caroline, and Joi—thank you for making our cul-de-sac safe and warm. Janice, we will miss you, too!

The female friendships painted in this and many of my stories are informed by the real people in my life.

Especially Sissy, Kara, Vicki, Lisa, Erin, Meagan, Amanda, Lindsey, Charlotte, Judy, and my mother. Thank you, wonderful women!

Ed and Eddie. Always, *ever* for you. And Winnie and Tuesday, too!

Made in the USA
Las Vegas, NV
24 November 2021

35185061R00138